"Chicken!"

Behind me the Truelanders waited. Each of them had passed the tests of bravery, so I suppose the ones who began to murmur "chicken" had the right. We'd already run the gauntlet with Truelanders on both sides armed with switches that raised welts when they found their mark. Then we'd been blindfolded, taken out into the woods, and after being spun around to throw off our sense of direction, deserted to find our way back.

"Come on, Luke," Jacob motioned with his arm for me to follow him. "You can't quit now."

Without answering, I turned my back on him and started up the small rocky cliff to where the Truelanders stood in a curving half circle.

Then the sneers began again.

"Chicken."

"Coward."

As I moved through the midst of them, they pushed and shoved me. I wanted to break and run, but instead I walked steadily on. I made no answer to their taunts. No answer could be made.

I knew there would be a price to pay ...

Other Avon Flare Books by
Ann Gabhart

FOR SHEILA

Avon Camelot Books

DISCOVERY AT COYOTE POINT
TWO OF A KIND

BRIDGE TO COURAGE

ANN GABHART

AN AVON  FLARE BOOK

BRIDGE TO COURAGE is an original publication of Avon Books. This work has never before appeared in book form.

AVON BOOKS
A division of
The Hearst Corporation
1350 Avenue of the Americas
New York, New York 10019

Copyright © 1993 by Ann Gabhart
Published by arrangement with the author
Library of Congress Catalog Card Number: 92-90415
ISBN: 0-380-76051-7
RL: 6.2

First Avon Flare Printing: February 1993

AVON FLARE TRADEMARK REG. U.S. PAT. OFF. AND IN OTHER COUNTRIES, MARCA REGISTRADA, HECHO EN U.S.A.

Printed in the U.S.A.

RA 10 9 8 7 6 5 4 3 2 1

BRIDGE TO COURAGE

Chapter 1

When I reached the beginning of the bridge, which stretched away from me into the darkness, I stopped. Clouds covered the moon and stars, but I still had no trouble making out the silhouette of the train track as it shot out into the air across the river, each railroad tie a solid shape in the gray-blue of empty space all around it.

I could hear the Truelanders whispering and laughing while they waited for Jacob and me to move out on the bridge. Jacob was already on the first tie that bridged the open air.

Rooted to my spot on the cliff with my heart pounding in my ears, I couldn't make sense of anything the boys or Jacob were saying. I heard only noise and no words I could recognize.

It was miles down to the river below. Miles. And I knew if I stepped out on that bridge, it was miles I would fall.

Behind me the Truelanders waited. Each of them had passed the tests of bravery, so I suppose the ones who began to murmur "chicken" and "yellow" had the right. These words penetrated the fog in my brain and made the bare, flat bridge in front of me waver and change shapes into a dozen bridges from my past.

"Don't be a scaredy-cat," Dad had said over and over when he made me climb the ladders ahead of him up to his bridges.

I'd stand with my eyes tightly shut and try to pretend I didn't feel the pull of the ground far below. The moment would always come when Dad would tell me to walk out onto the bridge, and I'd have to whisper, "I can't."

"Of course you can, son," he'd say reasonably. "I designed this bridge. It's solid and you aren't going to fall. There's nothing in the world to be afraid of."

"Yes, Daddy. I know, Daddy," I'd say, but my feet would be too heavy to move and my eyes wouldn't open.

Then the fussing and the shaming would begin, and he'd end up half dragging me across the bridge to get me over my "ridiculous fear of heights."

"Come on, Luke," Jacob yelled at me. "Let's go on and get this over with."

I shook my head a little, and the railroad bridge on its trestles high above the Black River came back into clear focus with Jacob standing on it waiting for me.

The bridge itself was narrow and graceful as it spanned the valley below, but its underpinnings were solid and substantial. The bridge was old, but trains still crossed it. I'd seen one once, splitting the air over the river and making the whole bridge shudder.

I swept my eyes quickly over the bridge again as my stomach knotted up. The air flowed around it everywhere, even up through the ties themselves. There were no railings along the edge of the tracks and no walkway. The bridge was designed for trains, not pedestrians.

That was what made it such a good test. The bridge was sturdy. There was no reason anyone should fall off it, and it wasn't really all that far across. Even if we walked extra slow, the whole trip couldn't take over twenty minutes.

Still nobody would really want to walk out on that open bridge, not unless they were dared or had something to prove. Jacob and I had something to prove. We had to prove we were brave enough to be Truelanders.

We'd already run the gauntlet with Truelanders on both sides armed with switches that raised welts when they found their mark. Then we'd been blindfolded, taken out into the woods, and after being spun around to throw off our sense of direction, deserted to find our way through the trees to the camp. Jacob hadn't liked the shadowy darkness of the woods, and I'd had to find our way and encourage him at the same time.

Now Jacob was standing on the end of the bridge trying to encourage me as we faced this last challenge. Across that bridge and back and we would be Truelanders. I couldn't see Jacob's face, only his shape suspended there half-on the bridge, half-off.

"You go ahead, Jacob," I said. "I'm going home."

"Come on, Luke." Jacob motioned with his arm for me to follow him onto the bridge. "You can't quit now."

Without answering, I turned my back on him

3

and started up the small rocky cliff to where the Truelanders stood in a curving half circle. There were twelve of them. Once we'd passed their tests of courage, Jacob and I were to have been the thirteenth and fourteenth. Now Jacob would be the thirteenth.

I looked over my shoulder at Jacob. He was halfway across the bridge, and the sight of him moving through the gray air high above the river made my knees weak.

Suddenly instead of everything being in a fog, each word, each movement, each sound around me became crystal clear. I imagined I could even hear a rock sliding down the cliff toward the river far below and then Jacob's footsteps out on the bridge.

The faces of the Truelanders were white circles above their dark clothes. For a minute they watched me without speaking, their silence louder than words. Then the sneers began again.

"Chicken."

"Coward."

"Run along home to your mommy, fraidy-cat."

As I moved through the midst of them, they pushed and shoved me. I wanted to break and run, but instead I walked steadily, impassively on. I made no answer to their taunts. No answer could be made.

I had known there would be a price to pay when I turned my back on the bridge, but there were some things a person could not do. And crossing that bridge was one of the things I couldn't do.

They followed me for a few steps, Willie and Mike skipping ahead of me to stick their feet in front of mine to trip me. An hour ago they had been friends.

4

Eric Harden called them off the way one calls off dogs. "Let him go," he said. "He's failed the test. We want nothing more to do with him."

I looked back at him. He was only a little taller than I was, but the difference in our heights looked greater as he stood above me near the cliff's edge. Beyond him Jacob had made it across the bridge and was turning around for the trip back. From somewhere I caught the faint sound of a train whistle drifting through the night air. I turned my eyes from Jacob to the white blur of Eric Harden's face. "What happens if a train comes?"

"Only a coward would worry about a train coming," he said.

He turned his back on me, and the other Truelanders followed his lead. With their faces away from me, they almost disappeared in the gray darkness.

I found the campsite without straying in the wrong direction once. I had an unerring sense of direction that was as strong here in the night with no stars or moon to guide me as it was in the bright sunlight of day.

After gathering up my sleeping bag and camping gear, I picked up a couple of the other sleeping bags and hurled them into the bushes around the campsite. It didn't make me feel any better, so I left the rest of the sleeping bags where they were and cut through the woods toward home.

I came out of the trees in a field scattered with large round rolls of hay that the gloom of night turned into sleeping monsters, but the trembling had long ago stopped inside me. Instead I felt drained and exhausted as if I'd just finished a long race. The tightness in my throat now had nothing to do with being afraid.

When I could see my house in the pool of light cast by the security light above the garage, I stopped walking. Our house was the last in the clump of houses that had pushed out into the edge of the country. Light still spilled out of the bay window at the back of the house, and I wondered, for the first time since Jacob and I had begun the test of courage, what time it was.

Not that the time really mattered. I wasn't planning to go home till morning anyway since there would be too many questions that I couldn't answer.

Dad was home for the weekend. He'd helped me get my camping gear together, proud that the Truelanders had invited me to join them. He didn't know anything about the Truelanders, but that hadn't mattered. The idea of a group of boys camping in the woods had smacked of adventure which in turn suggested courage. He wanted me to be brave.

I saw his shape move past the window. He was a big man, tall and strong, who thrived on challenges. He claimed he could throw a bridge over any river or road or canyon and went all over the country proving it.

From the time I could remember, he'd been trying to get me to share the thrill he felt up on a bridge. I only felt afraid no matter how much he talked about the freedom, openness, and magnificence of the high places.

Mom and I used to travel with him from site to site, a year, sometimes more in each place, but when I reached thirteen they decided I needed the stability of the same school. We'd been here at Oak Ridge a little over two years.

Mom and I both liked Oak Ridge. It was the kind of small country town Mom had grown up in, and I'd had no trouble making a place for myself in the band and on the academic team. I'd made more friends here at Oak Ridge High than I'd ever made at any of my other schools.

Jacob was my closest friend. We thought alike about most things. At least until the bridge.

I looked back in the direction of the river. There was nothing to see. I kicked out at the hay bale, and my toe sank into its soft end. Jacob could have come away with me. He hadn't had to go across the bridge.

I rolled out my sleeping bag on the side of the hay that was away from the houses. After I climbed into it, I stared at the sky. There was still no glimpse of moon or stars. The dark was blacker now, melting away everything except the rolls of hay nearest me and the little glow of light reflected up toward the sky from the houses on the other side of the hay bale.

When Jacob first brought up joining the Truelanders, he'd been so excited about being a Truelander that I had tried to mash down the funny feeling I had about the whole thing. But when he'd started talking about having to pass before you could be a member, I couldn't keep from asking, "Pass what?" I hadn't looked up at him as I plucked a blade of grass from beside my backdoor steps, where we were sitting, and waited for his answer.

"I don't know. Some kind of initiation, I guess.

Nothing to worry about," Jacob had said, suddenly jumping up to walk back and forth in front of me.

"You don't really know much about them, do you?" I leaned back and looked up at him.

"I didn't say I did. That's one of the things that makes it all so much fun. To be let in on the secrets, you know."

"But an initiation. They could do anything to us," I had said.

"You aren't afraid, are you?" Jacob had stopped pacing and peered down at me.

I had met his look and said, "No more than you are."

It had been true then. Jacob had been more nervous about the whole thing than I had been, perhaps because he wanted to be a Truelander so much. And he had made it sound like fun. A group of boys learning to survive in the woods, and playing their secret games by night instead of by day.

It turned out that I couldn't play their games. As I stared at the dark sky, I wondered what they were doing now. Was Jacob through with his tests? Was he a Truelander, passed and accepted into the group? He'd be a part of the secrets, and I wouldn't.

I shut my eyes on the night and tried not to think about it. Instead I listened to the muffled roar of the big trucks rolling by on the highway five miles away. Then a screech owl gave the mice in the woods fair warning that it was out hunting. Somewhere a dog barked three quick short barks.

I could have been there with Jacob learning the Truelanders' secrets if I had been able to walk across the bridge. There would be a price to pay for failing their test of courage, and not having

Jacob to hang around with would only be part of it.

I thought of Dad again and wondered where his new bridge was. He'd told me, but I'd forgotten. Maybe if I begged, we could follow him to the new site, wherever it was, and leave Oak Ridge behind. Preferably before Monday.

In spite of the sick feeling I had in the pit of my stomach, I smiled at the foolish thought of moving before Monday and was able, after a while, to doze off.

Three times I fell off the bridge, and three times I woke with a jerk before I hit the dark water below. Once I might have screamed. I wasn't sure. But if I did, nobody was around to hear me.

Finally, I fell into a sleep so deep that not even nightmares could disturb it.

When next I woke, it was daylight, and I was staring up into the face of the biggest black dog I had ever seen. He was standing stiff legged over me, a growl rumbling deep in his throat.

Chapter 2

I jumped a little, and the dog growled louder. With a whispered, "Easy boy," I began inching up out of my sleeping bag, but when the dog's growl became a menacing bark, I froze.

Just when I had about decided I'd have to stay stock still in my sleeping bag until the dog got tired of holding me there, I heard a girl calling, "Shandy! Where are you? Shandy!"

The dog's tail jerked back and forth at the sound of the voice, and he let loose several short, quick barks that made my ears ring.

"What have you got treed back there?" she said, her voice closer now.

I finally managed to ease into a sitting position up against the hay. The dog watched me, still growling, but he didn't go for my throat.

"Nice boy," I said softly, but the words were lost in a new flurry of barking.

Now that I was sitting up, I had a view straight into his enormous mouth, past his teeth, and down his throat when he barked.

"Oh," the girl said when she came around the hay bale and saw me. The dog took his eyes off me long enough to give her a sloppy dog grin and frantically wag his floppy tail.

I, too, looked at her and wished there was some way I could burrow out of sight under the hay. Of all the girls in the world, the last one I wanted to find me treed by a dog was Shea Ashburn. But of course it would be her. Her father owned this farm, this hayfield.

"Would you mind calling your dog off?" I said after a minute. Growling again, the big dog turned all its attention back to me. I glanced at him and then back at Shea.

Her mouth was twitching with a smile. "Why should I? You are trespassing."

I looked at the dog's bared teeth and said, "Then if you won't call him off, sic him on me and let's get this over with."

She laughed out loud, the sound as fresh and clean as the morning air. She herself looked that fresh in her bright red warm-ups with her blond hair pulled back in a ponytail. She came over and grabbed the big dog's collar. "Come on, Shandy. He's not so bad. We'll let him live this time."

"Thanks," I said as I crawled out of my sleeping bag and stood up. I could imagine what I looked like in clothes I'd slept in and with my hair sticking out in every direction.

Shea Ashburn. Why couldn't I have run across her in the field last week? Any time but now. I leaned over and began rolling my sleeping bag in a tight roll while I kept one eye on the dog who still looked as if he wanted a few bites of me for breakfast.

Dogs usually liked me, but naturally hers wouldn't. As I tied the strings just so around my sleeping bag, I tried desperately to think up something to say. Shea was keeping a polite hold on the dog's collar, and I could feel her eyes on me.

There was something special about Shea Ashburn that went beyond just pretty. I wasn't sure whether it was the way she was always smiling or the way her blue eyes sparkled. It didn't really matter what it was. I just knew I liked it.

I'd been watching her for weeks on the bus and at school wishing I had nerve enough to speak to her. Now with every opportunity to talk to her, I couldn't think of a single sensible thing to say.

In the end, I just picked up my stuff and mumbled thanks again before I started off across the field.

"Hold on just a minute, Luke Dillon," she called after me. "You're not going to walk off across that field to your house without telling me what you were doing out here sleeping in my hayfield."

With a smile on my face, I turned back toward her. The fact that I could still smile after last night was almost as big a surprise as her knowing my name. "Or what?" I said. "You'll sic your dog on me?"

"I might." She didn't smile.

I retraced my steps to the hay bale and leaned against the end of it. "Okay. What do you want to know?"

She finally turned the dog loose, and he began sniffing the ground where my sleeping bag had

12

been. "Why you were sleeping here in the field for starters," she said.

"I was camping out." I ran my hands over my hair to smooth down the worst of it.

"Within sight of your house? Come on, Luke. That's for ten year olds." She looked at my pack and back at me. "I think you've been out with the Truelanders."

"You know about them?"

"That's all my brother talks about. The Truelanders this, the Truelanders that."

"He's not one of them, is he?" I ran back through the faces at the camp out again. I didn't remember Ray Ashburn being there.

"No, but he wants to be. He wouldn't hardly talk to anybody last night because he found out they asked somebody else and not him. That's one reason I came out with Shandy so early this morning. I was sick of being around him."

"Tell him he's still got hope. There's at least one spot still open."

"Then you were with them last night," she said, her clear blue eyes intently on me.

"For a while. I decided I didn't want to join them after all, so I left." The image of the bridge floated up in my mind, but I pushed it away.

"Why?"

"They wanted me to do something I didn't want to do." I could have gone on and told her. By Monday the whole school would know I'd chickened out, but today was Saturday.

For a minute, as her eyes narrowed on me, I thought she was going to insist on knowing what it was I didn't want to do, but then she leaned against the hay bale next to me.

13

"What do they do on a camp out?" she asked, not looking at me now. "I've heard all kinds of wild things, but nobody seems to really know. It's all such a secret."

"Nothing too bad," I said. "Of course, I didn't stay long enough to get in on all the secrets."

She pulled a straw of hay out of the bale and bent it into small sections. "I guess Eric Harden was there."

"He was there. He's the leader."

"Yeah, I know. Me and Eric were friends—you know, special friends—last year, but then he got into this Truelander stuff and all he could think about was camping out." She threw down the bent straw with a sigh. "Now I don't think you could say we're any kind of friends."

"His loss," I said without looking directly at her.

"Maybe," she said. "And I don't care about Eric anymore, but Ray and I have always been close. We're twins, you know, even though we don't look that much alike. I don't want him to go off and become one of these Truelanders and quit being my brother."

"That won't happen."

"How do you know?"

I shrugged a little. "I don't know. I don't have any brothers or sisters, but I imagine it's harder to quit being a brother that it is to quit being a friend."

She smiled. "Thanks. I'm glad Shandy treed you." Her smile disappeared, but her eyes stayed soft on me. "And I'm sorry about whatever the Truelanders did to you last night."

"It wasn't them. It was me," I said.

Her eyes searched my face. "Whatever it was, I'm sure you did the right thing."

I wanted to tell her about the bridge then, and try to explain why I couldn't cross it before she heard about it from the Truelanders, but I've never been able to explain how even the thought of being on a bridge makes me panic. So I didn't say anything.

After a few minutes she called Shandy to her. "I'd better get Shandy home in time for his breakfast or he might get mean on me."

"Yeah," I said.

She laughed. "He's really not so bad. Here." She patted her leg, and the dog rubbed up against her. "Here. He'll let you pat him now."

When I touched the dog's big black head, a warning growl rumbled in his throat again. I pulled my hand back.

"Shandy! Behave yourself." She looked up at me with a little shrug. "Maybe next time. See you." She began running back across the field, and the dog galloped along with her, running ahead and then doubling back to stay close to her.

Next time. I watched her till she disappeared over a little rise in the field before I turned toward my own house. I wondered if there would be a next time after the Truelanders told everybody about me and the bridge. They might not tell all their secrets, but they'd tell that one.

I trudged to the house in bright sunlight that didn't make me feel a bit better.

After stashing my camping gear in the garage, I slipped in the backdoor. I hoped nobody would be up, but the smell of bacon frying greeted me. I carefully wiped my face clean of feeling before I stuck my head around the corner of the kitchen to say hello to Mom. I was relieved when I didn't see Dad anywhere.

"Oh hi, Lucas." Mom glanced around at me. "I wasn't sure what time you'd be back this morning."

"Where's Dad?" I asked.

"Gone to the store to get the paper and some coffee. I can't believe I forgot to get coffee." She turned back to her skillet of bacon with a little frown.

"Dad won't care if you forgot the coffee," I said.

"I know." Mom sighed. "But he hasn't been home for a couple of weeks, and I wanted to have everything perfect for him."

Dad couldn't make it home every weekend. His new bridge site was too far away, and sometimes he had to work through the weekends if the work got delayed by the weather. At first, after Mom and I had settled in Oak Ridge, it had been strange not having Dad at home very much, but we'd gotten used to it. Now it was sort of strange when Dad was home.

On those weekends, Mom put up her typewriter and concentrated on keeping the house clean and cooking real meals instead of just throwing together sandwiches or heating pizzas. I stayed outside more shooting baskets in the goal Dad had put up after we moved here, and Abigail, Mom's newest kitten, stayed in the garage.

On Monday after Dad went back to his bridge site, I'd let the kitten back into the house. Mom would get out her typewriter and spread her pencil-marked pages all over the dining room table in front of the bay window, and things would go back to normal.

"I've got to wash up," I said now, and slipped off to the bathroom upstairs before Mom could stop worrying about the forgotten coffee long enough to ask me about my camping trip.

She hadn't really wanted me to go. "What if it rains?" she'd said yesterday afternoon before I left.

"Then he'll get wet," Dad had said shortly. "It won't hurt him to get wet."

Mom had wrung her hands and kept herself from saying all the other what-ifs that I knew were running through her mind. One of them might even have been "what if he falls off a bridge."

Mom had a great imagination, but she used too much of it to worry. She didn't just worry about me. She worried about her writing, too. She'd get halfway through a story and then worry that it wasn't good enough, and she'd stuff it away in a folder and start on something new. She had a big box of those folders in the closet.

Since we'd been at Oak Ridge, she'd been working on a book, and while she hadn't finished it, she hadn't quit on it either. She said this was the best place she'd ever had for writing.

I looked at myself in the mirror of the bathroom and thought there wasn't much chance she'd want to pack up and move before Monday.

"That was a joke," I whispered to my reflection. "Smile."

But I couldn't pull up a smile even when I

ordered one, and after a moment, I buried my dirt-streaked face in the steaming washrag.

At breakfast, Dad wanted to hear all about the camp out, and Mom wanted to know how I got the scratch on my cheek and the bump on the back of my hand.

"I must have run into some tree branches in the dark," I said.

Mom frowned. "You might have put your eye out."

"It's just a scratch, Mom," I said as I dug into my bacon and eggs. I hadn't realized till then how hungry I was.

"Where'd you go?" Dad asked.

"Down in the big woods up from the river."

"You might have gotten lost," Mom said. "That woods goes on forever."

"Estelle," Dad said looking across the table at her. "Luke's a big boy now. He can take care of himself." Dad turned back to me. "Can't you, Luke?"

"Sure." I grabbed a biscuit and tried to change the subject. "Great breakfast, Mom."

Dad couldn't be sidetracked that easily. "When are you going again?" he asked.

I chewed slowly while I tried to think of an answer that wouldn't lead to more questions, but I was too tired to come up with a convincing lie. I ended up saying, "I don't think I'll be going any more."

"Why not?"

I shoved my scrambled eggs around on my plate while my appetite disappeared. "I decided I didn't want to be a Truelander. That's all." I pushed my plate back away from me. "If it's okay,

I'm going to take a nap. I didn't sleep much last night."

"But you haven't finished your breakfast," Mom said.

"Let him go, Estelle." Dad's eyes were on me. "He's tired. He can eat later."

The questions weren't over, but maybe by the time they started up again, I'd have some answers ready.

In my room, I switched on the radio, pulled my shoes off, and threw myself across the bed. I didn't know why I worried about telling Dad the truth. He already knew about the bridges.

I turned the music up louder and waited for Mom to holler at me that I was ruining my ears, but she didn't. At least not before I went to sleep.

When I woke up, I had a blanket over me, the radio was off, and the house was quiet. Downstairs Mom had left a note that she and Dad had gone out to eat and to a movie.

I wolfed down the hamburgers she'd left for me in the oven and then made a bologna sandwich to top them off. As I ate the sandwich, I wandered around the house wondering what to do. Any other Saturday Jacob would have been here, or I would have been over at his house. We'd have been watching football games or shooting baskets.

On TV the Bears were playing, but I couldn't keep my mind on the plays. After a few minutes I flicked the television off.

When I went out into the garage to get my basketball, Mom's kitten leaped at me joyfully.

"Poor Abigail," I said and picked her up.

"Don't worry. It'll be Monday soon, and you can take over as ruler of the house again."

Purring, she rubbed her soft head against my cheek. I liked this new kitten better than any other Mom had had. She was white with gray ears and tail, and a splotch of smoke-colored fur surrounded her bright blue eyes. The kitten's eyes were almost the same blue as Shea Ashburn's.

"That's how I'll sweet-talk her if I ever get the chance again," I said to the kitten. "I'll tell her her eyes are almost as pretty as my cat's."

I let the kitten climb up on my shoulder for the trip outside. Mom had had a long procession of cats of all kinds and colors. Something was always happening to them, or she had to give them away when we moved. Her last cat had just disappeared three months ago, but Mom never grieved over any of them very long before replacing them. She said she needed another live body in the house while she was writing.

"I'll have to keep that monster dog Shandy away from you," I said as I lifted the kitten down to the ground. "He could swallow you in one bite and not even know he'd had anything in his mouth."

The cat curled up in the sun while I put up a few shots at the goal, missing most of them.

I didn't know Jacob was there until he said, "Not got your eye this afternoon, do you?"

"Nope." I chased down the ball from a missed shot and dribbled back to where he stood. "You want to try?"

He missed, too. I caught the ball when it bounded off the rim, but I didn't shoot again.

I bounced it a few times before I said, "Did everything go okay last night after I left? They didn't take it out on you or anything, did they?"

"No."

"No train came?"

"No train came," he said as he dropped down on the back steps.

"Then you're one of them now." I sat down beside him, still dribbling the ball in short little bounces.

"Yeah."

"That's great. I know how much you wanted to be a Truelander." The word sort of hung in my throat, but I got it out.

Abigail came over to rub against Jacob's leg, and he stroked her head to tail several times before he said, "Why'd you leave, Luke? It was the last thing."

I let the ball roll away and leaned back on my elbows to stare up at the sky. "I just couldn't do it, Jacob. I guess like they said, I chickened out."

"But I'd have helped you." He rushed on before I could say anything. "You helped me in the woods. I'd have never found my way back to the camp by myself, and I could have helped you get across the bridge. It wasn't so bad once you were out on it."

"I couldn't have done it, Jacob. If I'd walked out on that bridge you'd have had to carry me off. I know. I've been on bridges before."

I could tell he was looking at me, but I kept my eyes turned away. "It won't be as much fun without you, Luke," he said after a few minutes.

21

"Maybe it will," I said. "And you won't be off camping all the time."

"No." His voice was so strange that I looked around at him. He looked sort of sick as he stared down at the ground and said, "They won't let me talk to you."

Chapter 3

"You're talking to me now," I said.

He shifted uneasily on the step and sneaked a look over his shoulder as if he thought somebody might be watching us before he said, "I had to talk to you once more anyway. To let you know what was going on."

I looked around, too, as though I expected the trees to sprout Truelander spies. "What's going on, Jacob? How can they keep you from talking to me if you want to?"

Instead of answering, he looked away from me, down at the ground.

"Oh," I said finally. "Well, I guess I'm supposed to say so long and it's been fun knowing you."

I started to stand up, but Jacob caught my arm. "I'm sorry, Luke. Really. I don't want us to stop being friends, but it's the only way I can be one of them."

"Then don't be one of them."

"But I have to." Jacob let go of my arm and stared at the ground again. "You don't understand. You haven't lived here in Oak Ridge all your life."

23

"So?"

"So my big brother was a Truelander. My uncle was a Truelander. All my cousins. I have to do it whether I want to or not."

In spite of myself I was beginning to feel sorry for him. He looked every bit as miserable as I felt. "It's okay, Jacob. I suppose I would have been one of them too, if I could have been."

"Yeah. But I don't think it's going to be exactly the way we thought."

"What do you mean?"

"I don't know. All the junk they had me do after the bridge, it just seemed sort of silly, and then the way they talked about you. I mean if you didn't want to go across the bridge that was your business." He was quiet a minute before he added, "I think they're afraid you'll tell all their secrets."

"I don't know enough of their secrets to tell, and even if I did, I wouldn't tell them."

"That's what I told them, but they wouldn't listen to me. And that's when they said I couldn't talk to you any more. None of us can. Willie or Mike or any of them. Eric decided that would be the best way. He said, well, he said a lot of things."

I attempted a smile. "I guess at least if none of you are talking to me, you won't be giving me a hard time either."

Jacob looked uncomfortable. "I shouldn't tell you this. They'd kick me out for sure if they knew, but I have to warn you."

"Warn me?"

"Eric's going to get Skeets on you. I don't know how, if he's going to pay him or what, but he said he'd take care of it."

"Skeets?"

"Yeah."

Skeets was the local tough guy at Oak Ridge High. They told all kinds of stories on him, and even if only a fraction of them were true, it was enough to make underclassmen like me and Jacob avoid him like the plague.

"He can't do anything that bad," I said. "Not at school."

"Yeah," Jacob said again, and I knew he was thinking about the time Skeets had doused a kid's head in the toilet and then made the kid beg him to do it again.

"I'll be okay," I said. "I'm not afraid of Skeets." I got off the step, grabbed the basketball, and began dribbling it first with one hand and then the other, my back to Jacob. "I'll just stay out of the restroom. Oak Ridge High won't be the first school I ever went to where it wasn't safe to take a leak."

Behind me Jacob stood up, too. "I'll help you if I can."

"Don't worry about it," I said. "I can take care of myself."

He didn't say anymore, and I concentrated on bouncing the ball as if the exact height of each bounce was the most important thing in the world. After a while, he left.

I let the ball drop and roll over into Mom's roses. Then I slumped back down on the steps. Abigail jumped up on my leg, but I didn't have the heart to rub her.

It was true what I'd told Jacob. I wasn't afraid of Skeets, not the way I was afraid of bridges. I could face him and take whatever he did to me, but I dreaded it.

Monday was every bit as bad as I expected. At a small school like Oak Ridge High, it didn't take long for the story to circulate. Whispers followed me down every hall, and when I went into a classroom a hush fell for just a moment as everybody looked up at me and then quickly away. Each time I heard a laugh, I was sure somebody was laughing at me.

Worst of all, whenever I chanced upon one of the Truelanders, they stared coldly at me before slowly turning their backs as though the very sight of me contaminated them. Jacob followed their lead, and although I'd told him I understood, I didn't.

As for Skeets, I passed him several times in the hall, but he paid no attention to me. I would have been less unnerved if he'd threatened to punch me in the nose. Then at least I'd have known what to expect. This way I had to imagine all sorts of things and keep waiting for them to happen.

Shea Ashburn was the only kid in the whole school who acted as though nothing weird was going on. "Hi, Luke. Are you ready for the algebra test?" she asked when she caught up with me in the hall before our last class. She didn't have to push anybody else out of the way. I'd been walking in my own private bit of space all day as everybody else kept their distance.

The algebra test was the last thing in the world I was worried about, but I played along with her in pretending that this was just another run-of-the-mill school day and said, "I think I know most of it."

"You would," she said with a laugh. "You probably didn't even have to study."

"I studied some." I didn't add that I hadn't had anything else to do, and I'd needed an excuse to hide away from Dad's eyes all day Sunday.

"I studied a lot, but all those formulas. I hate x's and y's."

"You won't have any trouble if you studied."

Smiling, she went into the classroom ahead of me. As I followed her, I decided having Shea Ashburn smile and make a special effort to talk to me was probably as weird as all my friends not talking to me.

The hush greeted me as it had in every other class. Shea was already in her seat with her eyes riveted to her book for some last minute studying. She paid no attention to me or anyone else. Her brother, Ray, on the other hand stared doubly hard at me.

They didn't look much alike. While Shea looked full of sunshine and energy, Ray looked too slim, almost pale. A frown traced small lines between his eyes as he kept staring at me.

I didn't know Ray very well even though we were neighbors. I'd been too shy to try to make friends with Shea, and Ray had always seemed to be absorbed in his own private world. I supposed he had friends, but I didn't know who they were. Maybe some of the Truelanders. Shea had said Ray wanted to be part of the club. I wished him luck, but if he wanted to be a Truelander, he'd have to learn to quit staring at me and turn his back instead.

After algebra class, Shea fell in beside me as we

hurried to catch our bus. "That wasn't so bad after all," she said.

"What?" I saw Jacob up ahead and slowed down so I wouldn't have to watch him turn his back on me again. "Oh, you mean the test."

"Of course. What else?" She was smiling. "I think I did okay. I hope Ray did. He has trouble with algebra, but he won't study with me. He says I think I know everything." She glanced over at me. "Maybe you could help him sometime."

"Sure, if he wants me to," I said, knowing he wouldn't.

"That would be great." She reached over and squeezed my arm a little. "I'll talk to him about it." She let go of my arm. "I've got to run to my locker. See you on the bus."

I watched her rush away, her hair swinging. Other people moved in around her once she was no longer walking with me. I couldn't keep my heart from speeding up a little even though I knew she'd only been talking to me because she felt sorry for me.

When I turned back around, I almost bumped into Skeets, who was just standing there behind me, staring off up the hall.

"Sorry," I mumbled and gave way to him. I'd never realized until that moment that Skeets was always alone, too. The other kids stayed at least one person's width away from him just the way they had with me all day.

His eyes settled slowly on me. We were about the same height, but he was at least twice as wide through the shoulders. Standing there in front of me, he looked like a solid mound of muscle. His slate gray eyes held no hint of warmth as he said, "Watch where you're going, kid."

"Sorry," I said again and moved to the side to pass him. I was acutely conscious of the kids stopping around us, standing well back, out of the way but watching and waiting.

He grabbed hold of my upper arm in a viselike grip. "I didn't say you could go yet."

"I've got to catch my bus." My voice came out calm, impressing even me. Inside my heart was beating so hard that it was making my toes knock together inside my shoes.

"Well, why don't you run then?" he said and shoved me enough to make me stumble.

I caught my balance and walked on toward the door, my eyes straight ahead. I didn't want to see the faces of the kids watching because I knew one of them was probably Jacob. Shea might even be back from her locker by now.

"You're not running, kid," Skeets said behind me. "I told you to run."

I acted as though I hadn't heard him and kept walking. Whatever happened, I wasn't going to run.

Nobody else was moving except to part in front of me and let me pass through them. The buses were waiting in front of the school. In a few minutes, right on schedule, the drivers would shove them all down into gear and roll away with or without their customary riders.

"You can run now or tomorrow," Skeets said, closer behind me now than he had been a few minutes ago.

I braced myself for some sort of attack while I kept walking right through the front doors where I could see my bus, number fifteen. I'd run to catch my bus dozens of times, but I'd walk home before I ran today.

Shea ran by with a funny little look back as she passed me. I kept walking. The bus was moving when I got to it, but the doors were still open. I climbed aboard and dropped into the first empty seat.

Only then did I look back at the school. Skeets was standing on the steps. The other kids flowed around him, but nobody touched him.

I stared out the window through all the stops and starts and wouldn't let myself even glance toward Shea though I had the feeling she was watching me. She would smile if I looked at her, but I didn't want her to talk to me just because she felt sorry for me.

So I kept my eyes on the houses and trees and tried to lose myself in another world. I'd been good at that once. I half-smiled remembering how I used to spend hours being Captain Masterson, the super hero.

My smile disappeared as I thought of the solid bulk of Skeets. Joseph Skeets. Nobody but a few teachers ever called him Joseph. He was Skeets. He was mean, and you did everything you could to keep from crossing his path.

As the bus approached my house, I stood up and began making my way forward. Shea and Ray were still on the bus, but I kept my eyes away from them.

"See you tomorrow, Luke," Shea called out when I passed her seat.

"Yeah." I glanced over toward her without really looking at her. "Tomorrow."

Tomorrow, Skeets had said, and though his voice had been oddly flat and soft, there'd been a menacing threat to it. *Tomorrow.*

I sighed as I went into the house, the dread of tomorrow building up inside me. I didn't see how things could change so much in three days.

At least things were the same at home. Now that Dad had gone back to the site of his new bridge over in the next state, Mom had her typewriter out of the closet and was pecking away.

"Oh hi, Lucas. I didn't hear you come in." She glanced over her shoulder at me, her mind still half on her story. "Your day at school go okay?"

"Sure, Mom. Great. How about yours?" I swooped up the kitten who'd hopped down from the windowsill to greet me.

"No writer's block yet. I'm on chapter ten."

"That's great." I walked on into the kitchen, wondering what she'd do if I told her about Skeets. I needed to talk to someone about what was happening, but of course I couldn't talk to Mom. She'd what-if the whole situation to death and end up having me with broken legs and arms or worse. My what-ifs were working well enough without any help from her.

With Abigail riding on my shoulder, I grabbed my basketball and went outside. Mom didn't even look around.

I put the kitten down to scamper through Mom's flowers and pounce on bugs while I attacked the goal with a flurry of shots from every angle.

The black dog knocked me sideways as he barreled past me toward the flower bed and then across the yard with Abigail only a whisker in front of him.

31

I yelled, but Shandy paid no attention to me. Yowling in terror, Abigail leaped the last few feet to the tree and scrambled up into its branches as fast as she could.

I ran to grab the dog's collar and pull him away from the tree, but as soon as I reached toward him, Shandy's barks turned to growls. My hand froze in midair.

"Shandy!" Shea came racing around the house and grabbed the dog. "I'm sorry, Luke. He didn't bite you, did he?"

"No, but I think my cat just had a nervous breakdown." I pointed up at Abigail who had stopped yowling and was now meowing pitifully.

"Oh, what a pretty kitten. What's its name?"

"Abigail."

We stared up at the kitten who hunkered down on the limb and stared woefully back at us.

"She looks scared," Shea said finally.

"I guess she's got reason. Imagine you were her size and Shandy was after you."

Shea laughed just as Mom stuck her head out the door. "What's going on out here? I thought I heard a dog barking."

I introduced Shea and her dog, Shandy, and then pointed at the kitten. "Shandy chased Abigail up the tree."

"Oh dear," Mom said. "What if she can't get down?"

"Maybe if I get Shandy away from here, she'll calm down," Shea said.

"I guess that would be the best plan," Mom said. "But kittens do get stuck up in trees sometimes. Lucas, you may have to get the ladder out and climb up to rescue her."

That said, she went back into the house to her typewriter. I stared after her wondering how she could have lived with me for fifteen years and not know me any better than she did.

Shea touched my arm. "I am sorry about Shandy. He just doesn't seem to behave very well around you."

"I only have your word for it that he ever behaves." I glanced down at the dog who promptly growled when he saw me looking his way.

"I didn't know you had a cat, or I'd have left him at home." Shea looked up at Abigail again and said, "Poor little kitty. Shandy's sorry."

"I'm not so sure about that," I said with a quick glance at the dog.

"He may have liked the chase, but he wouldn't have hurt the kitten if he'd caught her. He's really gentle underneath."

"Yeah, well, if you say so." I looked back up at Abigail. "I'll get her down somehow."

After Shea had dragged Shandy away from the tree and gone home, I tried coaxing Abigail down with words and even a can of her favorite cat food, but the kitten clutched the branch with a terrified, paralyzed stiffness I understood only too well.

Chapter 4

When Shea came back, I had the ladder propped against the tree. Abigail still sat frozen up on her branch, and I sat frozen on the ground.

I had tried to talk myself out of it while I got the ladder out of the garage. The ladder was strong, sturdy, and I wouldn't have to climb that high on it. And poor Abigail. I had to get her down.

It all sounded easy enough when I thought it through. I'd hop up the ladder, grab Abigail, and be down again before I hardly knew I was off the ground. I'd just block out the way I somehow connected ladders with bridges in my mind.

I had tried. I'd stepped on the first rung with no problem. The second and third weren't much worse. My heart was beating a little harder, but I told myself I was only imagining that I was scared.

Then as I tried to step up to the fourth rung, the stiffness entered my knees. My hands clenched the sides of the ladder, and sweat broke out on my forehead. I couldn't step up any higher, and several minutes passed before I could clear away my fear enough to be able to jump off the ladder.

Still shaking inside, I had just sunk down to the ground when Shea came around the house. Again, just like the day her dog had found me in the hayfield, I had looked at her and wished I could just disappear.

"Don't worry," she said when I looked at her. "I locked Shandy in the garage."

"Good." I tried to sound as if I meant it.

She glanced up at Abigail still in the tree and at the ladder leaning against the tree trunk, and then she looked back at me. I kept my eyes on Abigail as though I was trying to figure out my next move in the kitten's rescue, but I could feel Shea's eyes measuring me.

She dropped down on the grass beside me. "What's wrong, Luke?"

"Nothing," I said. "I just thought it would be better to give Abigail a chance to come down by herself, so that maybe she wouldn't be so scared the next time she was up a tree. I mean she'll surely come down eventually."

"I guess so."

An uncomfortable silence fell between us. I wanted to say something to get rid of it, but I could only stare at the ladder and imagine what Shea was going to think when I had to get Mom to come out and rescue Abigail.

After a long time, Shea said, "What was it the Truelanders wanted you to do that you wouldn't do, Luke?"

"Nothing much."

"What was it?" she insisted. "You don't have any reason to keep their secrets. Not after today."

"Walk across a bridge."

"The railroad bridge?" When I nodded, she

went on. "Well, I don't blame you. Nobody in his right mind would walk across that bridge."

"Jacob did. He said it wasn't so bad."

"Then why didn't you do it?"

"I couldn't."

"Why not?"

"I just couldn't, that's all." My voice sounded louder than I'd intended.

"You're afraid of heights, aren't you? That's why you wouldn't cross the bridge," she exclaimed as if she'd just made a great discovery.

"So what if I am?" I said and jumped to my feet. Up above my head Abigail meowed weakly, but I ignored her.

"It's all right, Luke. It doesn't matter." And before I could stop her she was halfway up the ladder and reaching for Abigail.

I watched her pull each of the kitten's paws away from the branch one by one, and I remembered the time on a bridge when the big foreman of the work crew had unwrapped me from one of the support beams.

My father had been yelling at me. I was embarrassing him, but I couldn't turn loose of the beam. Then as the big man had picked me up and carried me off the bridge, he'd told my father, "The boy doesn't have to cross my bridge. Not today. Not ever if he doesn't want to."

Shea scampered down the ladder as easily as she'd gone up it even though now she held the kitten in one of her hands. "Here you go," she said with a big smile as she handed Abigail to me.

"Now I guess I'm supposed to thank you."

"Well. . . ." Her smile faded.

I didn't let her finish whatever she was going to

say. "Abigail would have come down by herself. All we had to do was wait."

"You had the ladder out."

"And you proved how easy it is to climb it, didn't you?"

"I was just trying to help." A puzzled frown crossed her face.

"Help? That's a laugh. You and your dog, Shandy."

A touch of anger leaped into her eyes. "You don't have to be so mean about it! I didn't bring Shandy over here to chase your cat up a tree on purpose. I just wanted to talk to you, to see if I could help you with whatever was going on with those crazy Truelanders."

"Nothing's going on. Everything's fine," I said. I tightened my grip on the kitten without realizing it. Abigail yowled and raked her claws across my hand.

"I don't know why you're mad, Luke. I was just trying to be nice," Shea said.

"I don't need any favors."

"Are you sure about that?" she asked, glaring at me.

I just glared back at her a minute before I turned away and went in the house. As soon as the door shut behind me, my anger drained away. I wanted to go back outside to try to catch Shea before she left, but my pride stopped me.

I dropped Abigail to the floor roughly. The kitten caught herself, recovered her dignity, and retreated to the safety of Mom's windowsill without a backward glance at me.

"Oh good," Mom said. "You got Abigail down. She'll think twice before she goes up a tree again."

"Not if Shandy's after her," I said.

"Is that dog still here?" Mom asked.

"No. Shea took him home."

"I'm glad to hear that. I never saw such a big dog. What kind is he anyway?"

"I don't know. A mixture probably."

Mom hit a couple of keys on her typewriter. "I'm almost through with this page, and then I'll get us something to eat."

"That's okay," I said. "I'm not really hungry."

As I climbed the stairs to my room, I kept seeing the way Shea had looked at me before she left. She'd never speak to me again. Nobody would ever speak to me again at school. Nobody, of course, except Skeets.

The next morning I was tempted to stay home sick. In truth, I did feel sick. My stomach was queasy, and my throat tight. But with a sigh, I pulled on my clothes, combed my hair down, and brushed my teeth.

Mom drove me to school every morning. She liked getting out, driving through the little town, and watching it wake up. She said she needed to see a slice of real life before going back home to immerse herself in the pretend lives of her characters.

Twice on the ride to school that morning, she asked me if I was feeling all right. "You look pale," she said.

"I'm okay. Just sleepy."

"You should go to bed earlier."

"I suppose so."

She gave me another look as if she wanted to say more, but then she switched off on another subject. "That girl with the dog yesterday. Shea. She was cute."

"Sort of," I said. I didn't want to talk about Shea or being sick or anything else. I just wanted to get to school, make it through the day, and get back home.

"Why don't you invite her over some time to watch movies with you or something?"

"She probably wouldn't want to come."

"She might. She was friendly enough yesterday." When Mom glanced over at me, I couldn't miss the gleam in her eyes. She was inventing a romance for Shea and me.

"Shea's nice to everyone," I said.

"But you don't think she could be interested in you. Is that what you're trying to say?" Mom didn't wait for me to answer. "You sell yourself short, Lucas. You're a nice looking boy, and I thought she definitely acted interested."

"Oh, Mom. You think every girl I meet is interested in me."

"There's no reason they shouldn't be," Mom said as she pulled up in front of the school. "You're a great kid, Lucas."

"Yeah, sure," I said. Then with a quick goodbye, I got out of the car and slammed the door shut before she could say anything more.

After she drove away, I forced myself to go straight up the steps in spite of the sinking feeling I had that Skeets would be waiting to jump me just inside the doors. Yanking up my nerve I pulled the door open and went inside.

Before I left home I had worked it out so that I'd barely get to school on time. Now, as I went through the door and looked both ways to see if anyone lay in wait for me, the first bell rang.

I had lain awake half the night planning every step I would take during the day. I had tried to think up everything that Skeets could possibly do to me and come up with a counter move to somehow prevent it, or at least come through it with as few injuries as possible.

A note waited for me on my locker. "Meet me at the old tennis courts after school if you're not chicken. Skeets." The words were printed boldly across the sheet.

I folded the note and stuck it in my pocket. I didn't have time to worry about the note now. I had to run for my first class. I barely made it before the tardy bell just as I'd planned. I'd been in such a rush that I hadn't even had time to notice if I passed any of the Truelanders.

I had seen Shea. She'd looked at me, but she hadn't smiled as she hurried past to her own class. I didn't know what I had expected, but I wished I could somehow erase yesterday afternoon and start all over again.

I had mapped my courses between classes so well that I didn't even see Skeets until just before the last period when he clubbed my books out of my hands with a casual blow. Then as I scrambled around picking them up, he planted a foot on my algebra homework. I stood up without attempting to get the paper out from under his foot.

When I started past him, he clunked the heel of his hand against my shoulder and said, "Hey, kid, don't you want your paper?" He lifted his foot off of it. "Looks important."

"No." I stared straight at him, making my eyes

as blank of feeling as his were. I reached into my pocket and pulled out the note I'd found on my locker that morning. "And you can have your note back, too." I let it fall down by his foot.

It was so quiet around us that I imagined I heard the note hit the floor. Skeets looked at the folded piece of paper, then back at me. Something flickered through his eyes as he glared at me. "Later, kid. Later." He dropped his hand, but leaned his shoulder over to bump me when I passed him.

I kept the blank look on my face and found my seat. A few minutes later, Shea came down the aisle and dropped my homework paper on my desk.

"I found this out in the hall," she said. "I thought you might need it."

"Thanks," I said as I brushed at the footprint Skeets had made on the paper. I looked up at her, keeping my eyes as blank as possible even though Shea's eyes, her whole face, showed she was willing to be my friend even if everybody else wasn't. All because she felt sorry for me.

As I kept staring at her without smiling, a wounded, hurt look crept into her eyes that made me ashamed of myself. Still I let her turn away without even trying to stop her.

All through algebra class as Mrs. Ballester tried to explain the problems, I kept sneaking looks over at Shea, but I never caught her looking my way. I didn't blame her. She'd tried to be nice. I hadn't.

After class I caught my bus and rode home without any problem, and without so much as a glance from Shea. I wouldn't have to worry about her and her dog showing up in my yard that after-noon.

Wednesday and Thursday went by pretty much the same as Monday and Tuesday. I found a new note in my locker every morning, each one sounding a bit more threatening. I read them and threw them in the first trash can I came to. I had no intention of meeting Skeets anywhere. Not even in the halls at school if I could help it.

But I did cross his path several times, and once or twice he appeared out of nowhere as if he'd been lying in wait for me. He didn't really do anything. Once he shoved my face down in the water when I was getting a drink at the water fountain. Another time he clipped me from behind and made me fall down. Nothing I couldn't brush off and continue on to class, my face as stony as his.

I couldn't fight him. Not only would he have been able to kill me with very little effort, but I didn't like hitting people.

Once at a school I'd forgotten the name of, I'd bloodied a kid's nose. The kid's name was Billy, and for a week he'd been grabbing my pencils and breaking them. One day at recess I'd told him to stop bothering me, and when he'd laughed at me, I'd punched him right in the nose.

Billy had been too surprised to hit back at first and then too scared by the blood gushing out of his nose.

Mom had gone pale when she heard about it, but Dad had clapped me on the back proudly and said, "That's right, Luke. Stick up for yourself."

He wouldn't be so proud of me now if he could see me walking around Skeets and picking up my books without a word when Skeets knocked them out of my hands and avoiding the restrooms. But then Dad hadn't been proud of me for a long time.

Still I was fighting the only way I could by pretending none of it bothered me. All I could do was ride out the storm and hope the kids and Skeets would get tired of the game.

By Thursday afternoon a few kids did seem to be forgetting as they jostled against me in the hall. A couple of the Truelanders even forgot to turn their backs when they saw me.

That afternoon on the bus, I tried a half-smile of apology at Shea when I walked past her seat. Not waiting to see if she would smile back, I hurried on down the aisle, but after I took my seat, she turned around and looked back my way. Although she didn't really smile, she didn't look so mad anymore either.

The next morning I felt better than I had all week. The thought of Skeets no longer made me shake inside. I'd faced him all week and survived. The other kids were beginning to forget why I had to be avoided, and best of all I'd decided to apologize completely to Shea for acting like such a jerk the day she'd rescued Abigail from the tree.

She'd forgive me. She'd give me a second chance. And even if she had started talking to me because she felt sorry for me, maybe she'd keep talking to me because she liked me. Maybe with a little more time, Jacob might even get brave enough to start talking to me again once the excitement of being a Truelander dulled a little.

I felt even better when I saw no new note stuck

to my locker. Almost smiling, I worked the combination on my locker.

Then I pulled open the door, and a long black snake flopped out on my shoes.

Chapter 5

I couldn't keep from jumping back, but I did manage not to scream or yell which was better than some others were able to do as panic broke out around me.

Of course the snake was dead. I realized that almost as soon as it hit my feet. Still that didn't make me feel much better as I stared down at it. Someone had put it in my locker.

The note taped to the back of my locker door was signed Skeets the same as all the other notes, but I knew Skeets hadn't done this. Only one person knew my locker combination besides me, and that was Jacob.

I glanced around at the kids who were edging closer to stare at the snake and at me. I didn't see Jacob or any of the other Truelanders, but I knew they were watching from somewhere.

"What are you going to do with it?" a girl whispered, her wide eyes glued to the snake.

"What were you doing with that in your locker anyway?" someone else asked.

"He didn't put it there, dummy," another person

answered. "He wouldn't booby trap his own locker."

Their words circled around me while I stared down at the snake. I wasn't afraid of snakes the way I was of bridges. Even so, the only time I'd ever touched a snake was at a zoo, and that was a quick touch with only the tips of my fingers.

I took a deep breath, reached down, and grasped the snake behind the head. Its limp body hung down below my knees as I held it straight out in front of me and walked down the hill. Everybody gave me plenty of space, including Skeets.

"What are you doing with that, kid?" he asked as he stepped well out of the way.

"You should know. The note that came with it had your name on it." I stopped and turned to face him, the snake dangling between us.

"Not my name, kid." He backed up even more.

"Here." I held it out closer to him. "Why don't you take it back? That way I won't have to go to all the trouble of trying to explain the whole thing to the principal."

"I didn't have anything to do with that snake, kid." Sweat popped out on his forehead as he shrank back against the wall. Something close to panic began to show through the blank shield he always kept over his eyes.

For a minute I toyed with the idea of throwing the snake at him, but there was something too familiar about the look in his eyes. Turning, I went on down the hall toward the principal's office.

"Don't say I had anything to do with that, kid. Not if you know what's good for you," he called after me, the threat back in his voice.

I almost whirled and hurled the snake back at

him then. I was tired of being threatened and pushed and shoved. But just at that moment I caught sight of Eric Harden. He looked at me and smiled a little before he turned his back, and I remembered who my real enemy was.

I didn't go to the principal's office after all. A snake falling out of my locker would have been too hard to explain. Instead I stopped at the biology room where Mr. White, who'd been teaching too many years to be surprised by anything, was glad to take the snake off my hands.

"He's a lovely specimen," he said as he curled him into a jar. "I'll fix up some preservative for Wesley. Don't you think he looks like a Wesley?"

He waited for me to nod before he went on. "You know some of my students have never seen a live snake out in the wild. Never, and that's a real shame because snakes are lovely creatures. What happened to poor Wesley here?"

"I don't know. He was dead when I found him."

"You don't say," Mr. White said, his interest growing. "And where was that?"

"He fell out of my locker this morning."

He looked from the snake to me and raised his bushy gray eyebrows. "A joke, I suppose?"

"I guess you could call it that."

"Somebody is laughing, but not you?"

"Not me."

"Ah well, Lucas, we have the snake to add to my collection and that is good. Sometimes it is better to laugh and forget about things like this. Your practical jokester will tire of his game soon enough."

"Maybe," I said.

I knew what Mr. White was trying to tell me,

47

but I was too mad to listen. The anger that had been building in me all week had erupted, changing me until hitting somebody didn't sound so awful any more and I forgot to worry about Skeets even though he was everywhere I turned the rest of the morning.

He didn't touch me, but there was no mistaking the look on his face that said he was just waiting for his chance. I'd embarrassed him with the snake. He wouldn't let me get away with that.

Any other time I'd have been terrified at the thought of what he intended to do to me, but today I hardly gave it a thought except to wonder if he was skipping his classes to follow me around. Skeets had taken a back seat in my mind. As big and mean as he was, he could no doubt destroy me with one blow, but I'd worry about that when I saw the blow coming. Right now I was too busy searching the halls for Truelanders as I went from class to class.

At lunch I spotted the Truelander I'd been watching for. As Jacob began turning his back to me, I moved around in front of him. He met my eyes for a brief second and then stared at the wall.

"You gave them my combination," I said.

He looked a little sick, but he didn't say anything or shift his eyes from the spot on the wall.

"Tell your friend, Eric, that I'm not afraid of snakes," I said.

"I didn't know about the snake, Luke. Honest. They just said a note." Jacob's eyes flicked from the wall to me and then back to the wall again. "I didn't think you'd pay much attention to a note, and they told me I had to prove my loyalty. You understand, don't you, Luke?" His last words were almost a whisper.

"No," I said and walked away. He was still standing there staring at the wall when I went in the cafeteria with Skeets three steps behind me.

After I got my tray, I looked around for a place to sit. Skeets had sat down at the end of a table with empty chairs all around him. I thought about joining him, but I decided I didn't want to stay in Oak Ridge High's Siberia. So without the slightest hesitation I plopped my tray down in an empty spot at a table crowded with kids and sat down.

Everybody at the table stopped eating for a moment and looked at me. Then a boy named Steve picked up his tray and moved to another table. He wasn't a Truelander, but maybe like Ray Ashburn he had hopes of being recruited. Nobody else moved while I ignored them and began eating.

After a minute, a girl named Cathy broke the uneasy silence. "What did you do with it, Luke?"

I looked up at her as though I didn't know what she was talking about.

"The snake," she said. "I saw you carrying it down the hall."

"I gave it to Mr. White. He named it Wesley and put it in one of his display jars. You can go by his room and look at it if you want to."

"No thanks," Cathy said with a shiver.

"Who put it in your locker?" a boy sitting across the table from me asked. "I heard it was Skeets."

I opened my milk carton and stuck my straw in it. "Skeets wouldn't bother with snakes. He'd just hit me and get it over with."

"Yeah, or dunk your head in a toilet," somebody added from the other end of the table with a laugh.

"Then who did put it there?" the boy across the table persisted.

"Maybe nobody. Maybe poor old Wesley just crawled in there on his own, took one sniff of the gym clothes I forgot to take home last week and choked to death on the smell."

Several kids laughed before normal talk resumed around the table. They all knew the Truelanders had branded me a coward and an outcast, but they were talking to me anyway. Maybe I didn't have to stay an outcast after all.

On the bus that afternoon, Shea stopped at my seat long enough to say, "Why don't you come over later?"

She looked at me as though she expected me to refuse, but I surprised her. "Sure. What time?"

"Any time." Then she went on back in the bus to sit by Ray. I glanced back at her and saw Ray frowning as he said something to her, but she wasn't paying much attention to him. When she saw me looking at her, she smiled.

Dad wasn't home, and Mom was so engrossed in chapter eleven that she looked surprised to see me when I came in the door.

"Oh, I didn't realize it was that late," she said.

Abigail came to wind around my legs, and after I stroked her a few times, I said, "I think I'll take a walk if I've got time before supper, Mom."

She glanced around from her typewriter again. "Sure, go ahead. When you get back we'll get a pizza or something. Your father's not coming in this weekend."

The relief that flooded through me was quickly

followed by shame that I didn't want to see Dad. Still, if he didn't come home, he couldn't find out about the bridge or the Truelanders.

I walked straight across the hayfield toward Shea's house. Mr. Ashburn had moved all the round bales of hay over to a long line at the fence row, and now the field lay open and green before me. Running a little just for the fun of it, I watched my shadow jog along beside me.

My father had once accused me of being afraid of everything, even my own shadow. In a way it was true. I had been afraid of the way my shadow sometimes fell off the side of the bridges. I'd been afraid the shadow might drag me over with it.

Then I'd come up with Captain Masterson, and when my shadow fell over the side of the bridges, it was only Captain Masterson parachuting down to safety or playing hide-and-seek. In the early morning or late evenings I'd stand with my back to the sun and let my shadow stretch away from me, tall and big. That's when it was the most fun being Captain Masterson.

For a second I wished I could use Captain Masterson now against the Truelanders or Skeets, but then I laughed at the silly thought. Captain Masterson wasn't real. Skeets was. I shook my head a little and decided to stop worrying about any of it until Monday, especially about Skeets.

Besides, I was beginning to think his reputation was built more on rumors than actual happenings, because when I thought about it nobody knew who the boy was that had gotten his head doused in the toilet bowl or who it was that Skeets had pushed down the stairs or who had been threatened with broken fingers. Everybody knew the stories. Nobody knew any names. At least not until I came along.

Everybody knew my name. The story of the snake had gone through the school like wildfire, and in spite of what I'd said at lunch, Skeets had gotten full credit.

It was enough to make me almost feel sorry for Skeets. Almost.

Ahead of me, I saw Shea's house, and I pushed Skeets completely out of my mind. I'd figure out what to do about him next week. Now I just wanted to look forward to being with Shea. The last five days at school and Skeets and the Truelanders weren't important.

Shandy came bounding out to the end of the driveway to greet me with a ferocious flurry of barks. With him right at my heels, I expected to feel his teeth sinking into my leg any minute, but I kept walking toward the house.

"Shandy!" Shea came around the house and hollered at the dog which only made Shandy bark that much louder.

Then someone behind her whistled sharply. Shandy deserted my heels at once to run to the other person. Since I was looking into the sun, it was a minute before I realized that the boy wasn't Ray, but Skeets.

I shook my head and looked again, sure that my eyes or my mind had to be playing tricks on me, but it was Skeets stroking Shandy's big black head while the dog practically shook his tail off in ecstacy. I looked from him to Shea. She was the one playing tricks. From the look on her face, I could tell she'd planned this whole meeting.

"Hi, Luke," she said as though nothing was

wrong and Skeets wasn't standing there behind her glaring at me. Then with an innocent smile she glanced over her shoulder at Skeets and added, "You two know each other, don't you?"

Struggling to cover up what I was thinking, I met Skeets's cold eyes. "You know we do," I said. He nodded slightly and turned his eyes back to the dog who was pushing his nose against Skeets's hand.

Shea's laugh sounded a little strained as she looked from me to Skeets. "Sometimes I think Shandy likes you better than me, Skeets."

"We understand each other," Skeets said.

"He sure doesn't like me," I said. At the sound of my voice, Shandy threw me a look and a half-hearted growl before he turned his full adoring attention back to Skeets.

"He's a smart dog," Skeets said.

"Now, Skeets. He just doesn't know Luke as well as he does you." Shea smiled over at me. "Skeets works for my father a lot on the farm. Right now he's waiting for Dad and Ray to get back from town with the stuff they need to work on the barn roof this afternoon."

"Oh, I see," I said. "Well, I just came over to say hello. Guess I'd better be getting on back."

"Don't go yet, Luke," Shea said. "I thought maybe we could talk a while."

I just stared at her, sure she'd lost her mind. Skeets looked at Shea, too, and when he was looking at her, something changed in his eyes. The next thing I knew he was saying, "You live around here, Dillon?"

"Not far from here," I said.

Shea jumped in to stretch out my answer. "The

53

house just before you get here. You know the one with the big windows."

"Yeah. Nice house," Skeets said. We stared at each other a long moment. Shandy must have felt the tension between us because the dog looked up and growled at me again.

"Luke's got the prettiest cat," Shea said to break the silence between us.

"I don't like cats," Skeets said.

"I didn't know you liked anything," I said.

Shea stepped over between us as though she thought she could hold us apart if our words erupted into blows. Her eyes flew from Skeets to me and then back to him.

He kept his eyes on me. "I hear you don't like bridges."

"You could say that." I kept my voice even. "And I could say you don't like snakes."

His eyes got even colder on me, and if Mr. Ashburn hadn't pulled in the drive and tooted his horn at that very moment, I think he'd have knocked me flat even with Shea standing there between us.

Instead he pulled his eyes away from me and looked at Shea. Again the lines of his face softened the barest bit as he said, "See you later, Shea." Then he shoved past me to the truck, knocking his shoulder into mine. Shandy, following him, reached over and nipped my jeans.

"Behave yourself, Shandy," Shea said.

The dog hunkered down a few seconds at the sound of her voice, but then pounced on after Skeets to the truck. When Skeets climbed up into the back of the truck, Shandy jumped up beside him.

After the truck left, Shea looked at me and then at the ground.

"What is it with you, anyway?" I said. "Are you trying to be some kind of Miss Fix-it or what?"

Chapter 6

"I just wanted to help," Shea said softly, not looking up.

"Help?!" I said. "How? By getting me over here where Skeets could kill me without anybody to stop him?"

"I wouldn't have let him hurt you." Shea looked up at me.

"You? You can't even keep your dog from biting me."

"Shandy just snapped at you a little. He didn't really bite you."

"Yeah, sure. I guess those teeth marks were already in my leg."

A little fire came into her eyes. "Well, if you'd tried to be a little nicer, Shandy might not have bitten you and Skeets wouldn't have shoved you. I mean, you could have tried."

"I could have tried what? Being nice to Skeets? Is that what you're saying?"

"It wouldn't have hurt you."

"I can't believe this," I said. "I'm not the one following Skeets around threatening him. And I haven't done anything to your dog either. I haven't done anything to anybody." My voice rose until I was almost yelling.

We glared at each other for a minute before I went on in a quieter tone. "And I didn't invite myself over here either."

"Nobody made you come," Shea said.

"Then I guess I'd better just go home."

She didn't say anything, and I was left with nothing to do but leave. As I started walking away, I wished I hadn't said about half the things I'd said, but I didn't see any way of taking my words back now. It wasn't that anything I'd said wasn't true, but after all, Shea had been trying to help. It wasn't her fault that it hadn't worked out the way she'd planned.

By the time I got back to the hayfield, my feet were dragging. All I had to look forward to was a long weekend by myself.

Halfway across the field, I heard someone running after me. My first thought was Skeets, and my heart lurched as I wondered if I could outrun him. But it wasn't Skeets. It was Shea.

"Luke, wait up," she called.

I stopped and waited for her to catch up with me.

She was breathing hard as if she'd run all the way from her house, and it took her a minute to catch her breath. Then she flicked her eyes up to mine before she stared back at the ground and said, "I'm sorry, Luke. Can we try again?" Her blue eyes came back up to mine.

"You know your eyes are the same color as my cat's eyes." As soon as I said it, I knew it had to be dumbest thing any boy had ever said to any girl. And Shea seemed to agree because she just stared at me with a funny look on her face. I rushed on. "I mean Abigail has real pretty eyes."

Shea laughed, and I knew it was going to be all right. Somehow we were going to be friends in spite of all our wrong starts. "I'm flattered, I guess," she said. "Abigail does have great eyes."

I laughed too, and suddenly it was as if we'd never been mad at one another. She fell in beside me as we started on across the field toward my house.

"Do you have to go home right away, Luke?" she asked when we could see my house up ahead.

"No, I was just going home because I was mad."

She looked over at me and then away at the mounds of hay lined up along the edge of the field. "I guess you had a right. Ray says I'm always trying to arrange everybody's life and that I ought to mind my own business sometimes."

"Was that what he was telling you on the bus this afternoon?"

"Sort of," Shea said evasively. "But really, I was just trying to help even if I didn't do a very good job of it."

She turned for the woods, and I followed her lead. When we entered the shadows under the trees, I remembered going this way to the camp out just a week ago and how much had changed since then. "There are some things that nobody can help," I said.

"That's true only if you want it to be true." Shea jumped around in front of me where she could look into my face. "And I really wanted to help."

"How? By giving me and Skeets a chance to fight it out?"

"I didn't think you'd fight, and you didn't actually come to blows." She was standing in a spot of sunlight there among the trees, and although she wasn't smiling, everything about her looked bright and intense as she kept trying to explain. "You see, when I heard about the snake I knew for sure that Skeets hadn't had anything to do with that, and I thought if you knew that, too, it might help."

"I already knew Skeets hadn't put the snake in my locker."

"What do you mean? Everybody at school was saying he'd done it. They said there was some kind of note." She frowned a little as though my lack of disagreement upset her more than an argument would have.

I smiled a little. "Skeets isn't the note-writing type. He's more the hit you now and warn you later type."

"He's really not so bad," Shea murmured.

"And besides, he wouldn't have touched that snake, dead or alive."

"I knew that, but how did you know?" Shea asked.

"I know about fear. I thought Skeets was going to faint when I held that snake out toward him."

"I'll bet." Shea couldn't keep from smiling a little. "Poor Skeets. He tries to be so tough. He doesn't want anyone to know he's afraid of anything. But one day out at the barn a cow sucker wrapped around his arm, and Skeets almost jerked his arm out of the socket trying to throw it off. The more he jerked, the tighter the snake held on. Daddy had to yell at Skeets to get him to stand still long enough to unwrap the thing."

"That would bother anyone."

"I know. And anybody else might have laughed it off, but Skeets was so humiliated by the way he'd acted that he wouldn't come back to work for Daddy for months."

Shea turned and started walking through the woods again. I matched my pace to hers. After a few minutes, she said, "I know you don't believe me because of the way Skeets has been bullying you, but really he's not so bad."

"You sound as if you almost like him," I said, not looking over at her.

"I do. He acts mean at school, but when he comes out to the farm to help Dad, he's different. He's gentle with the animals and really good with the cows and calves."

"Shandy certainly likes him," I said.

"He brought me Shandy a couple of years ago. Shandy was the scrawniest, most pitiful looking pup you'd ever want to see. Skeets had found him on the road somewhere."

"Why didn't he just keep the dog himself?"

"I think he wanted to, but they don't have much yard space there at the trailer park and even then with Shandy hardly bigger than my hand, Skeets knew he was going to be a big dog. So I kept Shandy, but he still belongs to Skeets, too."

I walked along beside her without saying anything for a few minutes. I didn't exactly like what

I was thinking, and I wished I could just concentrate on the trees and the birds we could hear singing. The day was pretty, the place was pretty, and the girl with me was especially pretty. Why couldn't I just enjoy it instead of ruining it all by saying what I knew I wasn't going to be able to keep from saying?

As the ground began to slope downhill toward the river, I blurted out, "You like to collect strays, don't you?"

"Strays?" She looked around at me with wide, puzzled eyes. "I don't know what you mean."

"Don't you? Last week when I still had friends you didn't even notice me. Now this week, when I'm on everybody else's blacklist, you can't wait to be my friend or whatever."

Shea's lip trembled. "You're meaner than Skeets ever thought about being."

She whirled away from me and ran back through the trees but in the opposite direction from the one we had come. As I watched her, I felt like scum.

No sooner had she disappeared from sight than I knew I had to stop her and apologize. So this time I ran after her. "Wait, Shea."

It took me a while to catch up with her, because she kept darting in and out among the trees, ignoring me as I ran along behind her. Finally I took a chance, cut through the trees, and came out in front of her. Then all I had to do was wait and hope I'd guessed the right direction. I couldn't see how she could get back to her farm going this way, but maybe she knew a different route than I did.

When I heard her coming, I stepped back behind

some bushes. I didn't want her to run off in the other direction before I got a chance to apologize.

Now that she couldn't see me behind her, she'd slowed to a walk. When she rubbed her hands across her cheeks and I realized she was crying, I felt worse than scum.

For a minute I thought about staying hidden in my clump of bushes, but then I stood up and let her see me. I was relieved when she kept walking toward me instead of turning and going the other way.

When she stopped in front of me, I looked at her tear-streaked face and said, "You're right. I'm mean."

She nodded without saying anything.

"I'm sorry. I wasn't trying to make you cry," I said and gently touched her cheek with the tips of my fingers to brush her tears away.

She met my eyes and half smiled. "It's okay. Ray says I cry too easily anyway."

I moved my hand to her other cheek and brushed the tears away on that side, too. Then without thinking about what I was doing, I let my hand slip around to the back of her neck and pulled her toward me as I touched her lips with mine.

When I pulled away, I don't know which of us was the most surprised. Me or her.

"I'm sorry," I stammered, not sure if she was going to be mad or not.

She laughed. "The trouble with you and me, Luke Dillon, is that we can't stop apologizing to one another. 'I'm sorry' has made up half of what we've said to each other today."

I laughed, too. I wanted to lean down and kiss

her again. I believed I could do it better the second time around, but she dropped her eyes away from mine and said, "Besides, I'd rather you weren't too sorry."

I studied the top of her head. A few long blond strands of hair had pulled loose from the clasp she used to keep it all pulled back from her face. "I lied," I said. "I'm not sorry at all about kissing you. Just about being so mean."

"You're not really so mean," she said as she reached over and took my hand. We began walking again.

The birds' singing sounded sweeter, and the bright spots of sun that inched down through the branches felt warmer. Maybe being one of Shea's strays wasn't so bad after all.

As if she'd read my thoughts, she said, "You were sort of right about me collecting strays, I guess. Ray's always telling me I never like anybody unless they need me to help them." She looked up sideways at me. "But unless you count Shandy licking my face, I've never let one of my strays kiss me before."

All at once, the thought of Eric Harden popped into my head. He was anything but a stray. She'd probably kissed him dozens of times. I pushed the thought of Eric away. Stray or not, I was the one who was here with Shea now, holding her hand and walking toward the river.

We were close to where the Truelanders had camped out the week before, and I hoped we wouldn't run up on any of them in the woods. I didn't want anything to spoil this moment.

But as she kept walking farther and farther away

from my house and her farm, I finally asked, "Where are you going?"

"Why, home, of course."

"You must be taking the long way around," I said as I looked around us. "The river's just over there." I pointed.

"Are you sure?" She looked around at the trees and frowned.

"Yeah. This is about where we camped out the other night."

"Oh dear. Then I guess I'm lost again. I get turned around on my directions every time I go very far in these woods." She looked at me. "What are we going to do?"

I had to laugh at the worried look on her face. "Well, whenever you want to go back, we'll just turn around and go back."

"You make it sound simple, but I don't know which way to go."

"I know the way back."

"You do?"

"Sure. We just need to head back east."

"But how do you know which way's east?" Shea said.

"That's easy enough. You just follow your shadow."

She stepped over into a spot of sunshine, looked at her shadow and pointed east. "But the sun will go down soon. It's getting late already. What will we do then?"

"I'll still know which way's east."

"How?"

"I don't know, but I always have. I used to have to help Mom find the way around when we first moved to a new town. She used to tell me boys just have a better sense of direction than girls."

"I don't know about that. Ray isn't much better at directions than I am." She looked back toward the east and then the other direction. "It's sort of late, but if we're close, let's go on to the river for a few minutes."

We came out of the trees onto a wide rocky ledge that sloped gradually toward the river below us. Just beyond us to the left was the bridge.

When Shea sat down on a broad flat rock, I wanted to suggest we start back home, but I didn't want Shea to guess how just being this close to the bridge was making my heart jump and my mouth get dry. So as I sat down beside her, I kept my eyes on the river winding through the valley below us while the bridge lurked on the edge of my vision.

"Does it bother you being up on these rocks like this?" Shea asked after we'd sat there a minute.

"No." I looked around at the huge boulders. "They look sturdy enough."

"So does the bridge," she said. I didn't look at her, but I knew she was looking down the river at the bridge.

"In a different way." I picked up a sharp pointed rock and began to scratch white lines on the boulder.

"I don't understand. I thought acrophobia meant you were afraid of all heights."

"Maybe it does. Maybe what I have is bridge-phobia, if there is such a thing." I looked up from the lines I had begun to join together to make ladders. We were high among the trees on a fairly steep cliff. Yet I felt in no danger at all of falling off. The ground was solid under me. I tried to explain. "A long time ago I used to be sort of afraid up high like this, but I got over that."

"How?"

I glanced over at her and then began scratching out ladders on the boulder again. "You'll laugh if I tell you."

"No, I won't."

It was quiet around us as I considered whether to tell her about Captain Masterson. I'd never told anybody about him, not even Mom who always encouraged pretend games. The sound of the rock scraping against the boulder was loud in the stillness as Shea waited for me to answer her.

The moment lengthened and became almost uncomfortable before I finally began talking. "Well, you see, I've never been very brave about anything, but I've always wanted to be. So when I was a kid I used to pretend I was this super hero type. You know the kind that can do anything. Conquer all odds. I pretended he was especially powerful on top of hills, so I used to climb hills, each one a little higher than the last, until one day I wasn't afraid of being up on a hill even when I wasn't Captain Masterson."

A hawk whistled shrilly, and I looked up to watch the bird swoop and whirl in the wind currents above the river. That's the way Captain Masterson had been. Free and strong, and able to ride the wind without fear.

"All that was just a game," I said aloud and stared down at the small rock in my hand before I threw it up in the air toward the hawk. It didn't even come close, and the hawk sailed on his way, undisturbed. "I was never very afraid of places like this anyway."

"It doesn't matter how you did it. The point is that you did do it. You overcame your fear." Shea scooted over closer to me and laid her hand on my arm. Her voice was excited as she went on. "If you could do it then, you can do it now."

"I'm a little old to play super hero."

"You wouldn't have to. All you have to do is face your fear of bridges gradually the way you did the hills."

"It wouldn't work." I was staring down at the river, but I was more aware than ever of the bridge there in the background.

"It will if you try." She tightened her hold on my arm. "I'll help you."

I looked over at her. The wind was playing through her hair, blowing some of the strands over to brush against my face, and bringing with it the sweet smell of her shampoo. Her eyes on me were intense, determined. I was tempted to kiss her again, but I wasn't sure she would want me to.

After a minute, she said, "You will let me help you, won't you, Luke?"

I thought about the bridges and how I knew she wouldn't be able to help and that I should say so. But the thought of being with her again made me say instead, "I guess it's worth a try."

For a second after she leaned over and touched my lips lightly with hers, I nearly believed that with her help I might actually be able to conquer my fear. Then when we stood up and turned to start home, the railroad bridge was directly in front of my eyes with the air flowing under it and over it and through it.

A tremble of fear swept through me, and I knew that not even for Shea would I ever be able to step out onto that bridge.

Chapter 7

It was nearly dark when we came out in the hay-field again. The shadows in the woods had been thick, but I'd had no trouble finding my way through them from the river back to her farm.

All the way she had talked of nothing except how we were going to conquer my fear of bridges. I didn't tell her I wouldn't be able to do any of it. I just listened without saying much.

When we came out of the trees, she said, "That was amazing. I'd have never been able to find my way back here without going the wrong direction a dozen times."

"You'd have made it home somehow," I said as I turned with her toward her house. "Shandy might have tracked you down."

"Shandy? That dog can't even stay on a rabbit's trail." Shea laughed. "But you don't have to go with me the rest of the way home. I think I can make it from here, and it's almost dark. Your parents will be worried about you."

"Dad's not home this weekend, and Mom probably hasn't noticed I'm not there yet." At least I hoped she hadn't, because if she had, she'd be playing her what-if game and have me lying some-where with a broken leg, or kidnapped by aliens, or worse.

"But it will probably be completely dark before you get home."

"I'm not afraid of the dark," I said.

Shea looked around at the deep shadows and shivered. "Everybody's afraid of the dark or of what it might be hiding."

Just then a crashing noise came from the bushes at the edge of the hayfield, and Shea jumped over close to me as a black form hurtled out into the open.

I put my arm around Shea and said, "It's just Shandy."

Shandy bounded across the field in three leaps and shoved his big black body between us, first growling at me and then licking Shea's hand.

"Shandy! You bad dog. You nearly scared me to death jumping out of the bushes that way," Shea said as she ruffled his ears.

His tail thumped against my leg, but when I tried a touch on his head, he jerked around with another warning growl. Still, I stood my ground and kept my arm partway around Shea.

She looked from the dog to me. "At least now you can go on home. Shandy will keep the bad guys away from me."

"The trouble is he thinks I'm one of them."

Shea laughed. "He'll make friends with you af-ter a while." She moved away from me, and I didn't see any way to try for a goodbye kiss even though I'd thought of little else all the way back from the river.

"See you tomorrow," she called over her shoulder

as she started jogging toward her house with Shandy bouncing along beside her.

With the memory of Shea's smile and touch fresh in my mind, I wanted to just sink down there on the ground and think about how good being with her had made me feel, but I could see the lights on in my house. Mom surely would have noticed that I was missing by now, so I kept walking.

I paid no attention to the dark closing in around me as I picked up my pace. I'd meant it when I'd told Shea I'd never been afraid of the dark. Nobody ever made me climb up ladders to look at bridges in the dark, and even when I used to have nightmares about the bridges, the dark was welcome when I woke because it meant the dream was over.

I was almost to the end of the hayfield when a shape separated itself from the last roll of hay and stepped in front of me. My heart leaped up in my throat.

"I've been waiting for you."

As soon as he spoke I knew it was Skeets. I tried to tell my feet to run, but they seemed to be stuck to the ground. Before I could pull them loose, Skeets reached out, grabbed my shirt, and yanked me so close to him that I could feel his breath on my face and see the glint in his eyes.

"Let go of me." I tried to sound calm and in control, but my voice came out in a squeak.

"Sure, kid, I'll let you go," Skeets said, twisting my shirt in his big fist to get a firmer hold as he pushed me up against one of the rolls of hay. "I'll let you go as soon as I'm ready to let you go."

I knew it was useless to struggle against him. So

I just stood there with the hay poking into my back and tried to glare at him the way he was glaring at me, but it did little good to pretend I wasn't afraid of him. He had to feel my heart practically jumping out of my chest under his fist.

"What do you want?" I managed to say, my voice not quite such a squeak.

He just kept staring at me, and even though I couldn't see his face clearly in the darkness, I could tell he was smiling. A chill passed through me.

I waited for what seemed like an hour before I broke the silence again. "If you're going to hit me, go ahead and get it over with." I stuck my chin out toward him.

Again another silence, this time broken by Skeets. "This is just a warning, kid, but one you'd better listen to and listen good."

I listened.

He shoved me harder against the hay, but I hardly felt the stick of the stems now. "Stay away from her. She don't need a coward hanging around her."

"Who?" I asked foolishly.

"You know who." His fist was rock hard against my breastbone, and his face inches from mine. I could feel the heat of his anger.

Then as suddenly as he had grabbed me, he turned me loose and stalked away. I stayed where I was, letting the hay hold me up until my heart began to slow its frantic beating.

After I drew in a couple of deep breaths, I pushed away from the hay bale. My legs still felt a little shaky, but I was happy to be all in one piece without any lumps or bruises.

Still, the threat had been real enough. I was sure of that. "Stay away from her," he'd said. Had Eric Harden told him to warn me away from Shea?

My face flushed hot with anger as I thought about Eric Harden. Strangely enough, I wasn't that mad at Skeets. He was just a tool Eric Harden was using against me.

And Eric knew how to use him. The snake in my locker had not been just for my benefit, but calculated to stir up more trouble between Skeets and me. My face got even hotter as I realized that Harden was now using Shea, too. She must have told him about Skeets and snakes.

I looked behind me at the solid bank of darkness that was the woods. The Truelanders were probably camped somewhere in the heart of that darkness, laughing at me and planning new torments for me.

When I stumbled over a rock on the ground, I picked it up and hurled it toward the trees. There was no satisfying crash or bang as it landed, only a soft thud as the rock fell short of the trees.

With a sigh, I went on across the field to my house. Abigail met me at the backdoor with a worried meow, but Mom only looked up from her typewriter to say, "Oh, hi Lucas. I guess you're getting hungry. As soon as I finish this page, we'll go get that pizza."

I stared at the top of her head bent over her papers. She hadn't even noticed that I wasn't there! It might have been better to have found her standing in the middle of the floor wringing her hands, playing her what-if game. After all, I had almost been a what-if. What if Skeets had decided to quit warning and start hitting?

"I'm sorry I'm so late getting back from my walk," I said. I wanted her to know I hadn't just been out in the yard all the time.

"That's okay, dear," she said, her eyes on the paper in her typewriter and her mind wherever her characters were at that moment.

"I kissed a girl and this guy threatened to break every bone in my body," I said in the same even tone.

"That's nice, Lucas," she said. "You'd better feed Abigail before we go for the pizza."

That night I had the dream for the first time since we'd moved to Oak Ridge.

I was on a bridge, and then without quite knowing how I got there, I was dangling off the side with nothing but air under my feet. Yet I wasn't falling. I was just there. Something held me up, but I didn't know what. Then I was falling, the air whooshing past me as I plummeted down toward the ground. I jerked awake before I hit the bottom.

After my eyes flew open, I stared wide-eyed at the darkness and tried to remember the last time I'd had the dream. Once I'd had it nearly every night, sometimes two or three times until I'd been afraid to go to sleep.

I told myself it was just the pizza or Skeets and his threats or the Truelanders and their taunts that had brought the dream back now. I took a couple of deep breaths while I tried to push bridges as far from my thoughts as possible. Instead I tried to think of Shea and the way I'd felt after I'd kissed her.

But when I thought about Shea, I couldn't keep from thinking about her enthusiastic plans to help me conquer my fears. She thought it would be easy. That all I had to do was try, but I had tried. Time and time again.

The bridges marched through my mind until I wasn't sure which of them had been real and which of them were only in my nightmares. It didn't matter how hard I tried, I was still afraid. I didn't see any way I could change that no matter how much I wanted to impress Shea.

I'd impress her all right. I'd impress her in all the wrong ways. She'd call me a quitter or worse, but I'd still have to tell her I couldn't carry out her plans.

With that in mind, the next morning I left Mom at her typewriter and walked back across the fields to Shea's house. The morning was beautiful with a hint of fall in the air. Already some of the leaves in the very tops of the maples were turning red and orange.

The night had been cool, but now the sun was bright and warm on my back as I started across the middle of the hayfield. I glanced over at the rolls of hay along the fence row and kept my distance. While I didn't think Skeets would be there waiting for me, I wasn't about to give him another chance to grab me if he was.

He might be at Shea's. There was every possibility that he'd be working for her father again today, but I didn't slow down even as his warning echoed in my mind. "Stay away from her."

I wondered, as I kept walking, what Skeets would do to me. I considered what a punch in the face would feel like. It wouldn't be pleasant, but I wasn't going to stay away from Shea. Not unless she asked me to, which after today she might do.

How had Skeets put it? "She don't need a coward hanging around her."

When I got to her house, she ran out to drag Shandy away from me before he could go for my throat.

Her hair was still damp from her shower, and when she leaned over closer to me to grab Shandy's collar, the smell of her shampoo made me a little lightheaded. She was smiling, talking to me, and fussing at Shandy all at the same time.

When she finally got the dog to stop barking, I started in on the little speech I'd rehearsed on the way over. "I've decided that this isn't such a. . . ."

"No time to talk now," Shea interrupted briskly. "You're late, and Mama's in a hurry. We've been waiting for you."

"Late?" I said as I saw their slightly battered pickup truck coming around the house. It stopped in front of us.

"Yeah. We're going with Mama over to Whitton to get some roofing supplies Dad couldn't get in town yesterday." She gave Shandy one last pat on the head and climbed in beside her mother.

Totally confused, I climbed in after her. Mrs. Ashburn smiled at me and pretended that she hadn't minded waiting. Then we chattered on about school and the farms and houses we were passing. They paused to look at me every once in a while and politely let me put in a few words.

It wasn't until we were going down the hill to the highway bridge across the river that I figured out why I was in Shea's truck headed for the supply store in Whitton. She was testing me to see if I could ride across the bridge. I wondered if she'd be disappointed if I didn't panic.

Riding over bridges was different from standing on them. As long as the wheels kept rolling, I usually had no trouble at all riding across bridges. I'd learned to keep my eyes on the hood of the car, and sometimes I counted to ten slowly. Most of the time we were on the other side of the bridge by the time I quit counting.

I didn't have to count today. I was too conscious of Shea watching me out of the corner of her eye, and I worked so hard at pretending I didn't know what she was up to that we were over the bridge before I knew it.

The trip back with the roofing shifting around in the back of the truck was the same except that this time when we were over the bridge and started up the hill on the other side, Shea gave me a brilliant smile. I wished I had done something special to deserve it.

Back at the farm, Shea's mother got out of the truck, and Shea scooted over under the wheel. "Do you have your license?" I asked as shoved the truck into gear.

"Of course not. I'm not old enough, but I've been driving around on the farm for a couple of years now." She grinned over at me. "You afraid to ride with me?"

"I don't know. I'll tell you when we get there."

Shea laughed and headed the truck along a couple of dirt tracks through the field. I think she intentionally hit several dips that practically bounced me out of my seat.

When we could see the barn ahead, she stepped on the brakes at once and went the rest of the way slowly. She couldn't go slowly enough to suit me because I had spotted Skeets up on the roof along with her father. Ray, halfway up a tall ladder propped against the barn, began climbing down when he saw the truck coming, and Shandy appeared at the edge of the field to run along with us.

Skeets stopped hammering and stared at me when I got out of the truck with Shea. I stared back a minute before I went around to the back of the truck to help Shea and Ray unload the supplies.

Ray looked at me without speaking or smiling, and I half expected him to turn his back on me the way the Truelanders did at school. He probably would have if any Truelanders had been around to take notice.

After we had unloaded the supplies, Skeets called out to me. "Plenty of room up here for another hand, Dillon."

Mr. Ashburn smiled down at me. "Sure, Luke. Ray could use some help packing the stuff up the ladder to us."

I looked at the ladder and then up at the roof, and my heart fluttered. I wondered if Shea had planned this, too. Skeets and Ray were smirking at me, and Mr. Ashburn looked from me to them and back at me, his smile fading.

I cleared my throat and said, "I wouldn't make much of a hand. I've never down any roofing before, and besides I've got to be getting on home."

"What's your rush, Dillon? Need to feed your cat?" Skeets taunted me from the rooftop.

Mr. Ashburn frowned at Skeets. "If the boy says he can't work, Skeets, then he can't work."

"He can't work all right. That's true enough, right, Ray?" Skeets laughed, and Ray joined in.

I wanted to race up the ladder and knock Sheets off his perch there on the roof, but of course, I couldn't. I could only stand rooted to the ground while the word *coward* echoed over and over in my mind.

Since there was nothing I could say or do, I turned away from them and climbed back in the truck. I was grateful when Shea climbed in beside me and without a word started up the motor.

I didn't look at her as we drove away from the barn. I stared straight ahead with Skeets's laugh ringing in my ears.

Chapter 8

Instead of going straight back to the house, Shea stopped the truck in front of another, smaller barn. She cut off the motor, turned to me, and said, "You don't really have to go home right away, do you, Luke?"

I refused to meet her eyes. "I was just making excuses, and you know it."

"Good. That's what I thought," Shea said as she climbed out of the truck.

I thought it might be better if I did just go on home, but Shea was standing there smiling and waiting for me. So I climbed out after her and followed her into the barn.

The sweet smell of hay greeted us. On each side, square bales of dark green hay were stacked to the ceiling. "Alfalfa," Shea said. "Daddy mostly puts up his hay in the big round bales you saw out in the field, but he likes to put his alfalfa hay in the barn."

I half listened as she kept rattling on about the hay to fill up the silence between us, but once we'd found a seat on a bale of hay jutting out in the walkway, she stopped talking.

I leaned back against the hay. It wasn't as prickly as the hay Skeets had shoved me against the night before. "You'd better listen," he'd said. But I hadn't listened. I was here now with Shea, and just being this close to her made me feel a little giddy.

With our legs touching, I watched her out of the corner of my eyes. I wanted to move closer until our arms were touching, too, and then maybe even kiss her again. My heart speeded up at the thought, but I sat still. She wouldn't want to kiss a coward.

The look on her face seemed to confirm my worst fears as she scowled at the wall of hay across the walkway. The light was dusky in the barn, and the sounds from outside were muffled. If I listened hard, I could hear the faint tapping of hammers.

After we'd been sitting there for a long time, Shea said, "I just don't understand it."

I glanced over at her and then away. "It's not so hard to understand. I told you I couldn't climb ladders."

"No, no, I'm not talking about that."

"I'm sorry, Shea, if I disappointed you."

"What do you mean?" Her frown deepened as she looked around at me. "You think I planned all that?"

"Well, not all that. I don't think you coached Skeets on what to say." As she began to shake her head, I rushed on. "I know you meant well, but it's just not going to work. I've tried it all before. Dad saw to that."

The look on her face softened. "I didn't take you out to the barn so that you'd go up that ladder.

It was just a coincidence that Daddy was roofing today."

"You made sure I went with you and your mother so that I'd have to ride across the bridge with you."

She smiled a little. "I guess that was pretty obvious, but riding across didn't seem to bother you at all."

"If you'd wanted to know that, you could have asked, and I'd have told you. Besides, what would you have done if I had been afraid? If I hadn't been able to ride across the bridge?"

"I don't know. Helped you, I guess."

"How?"

"I don't know. Somehow."

She didn't have any idea about the kind of panic that seized me when I was on a bridge. I looked at her concerned face and hoped that she would never see me on a bridge. A chill went through me at the thought. It'd be better to stop seeing her at all than to let her see me the way I'd been the last time Dad had forced me out on a bridge.

She reached over and touched my hand. "You're not mad at me about it are you, Luke? I was just trying to help."

"I'm not mad," I said. "But I think we'd better just forget about all this other stuff."

"What other stuff?"

"The bridges and things."

"You can't give up already." She pulled her hand away from mine. "You have to try."

I didn't say anything, and after a second she went on. "You're just letting Skeets get to you." Her frown came back. "I still can't understand the way he acted. Skeets is rough sometimes, but he's not mean."

"Not mean?" I couldn't keep the amazement out of my voice. "Skeets? He works at being mean."

"Not really," she said softly, and then kept talking so I couldn't argue the point. "And Ray. Ray's just acting so different here lately. Sometimes I think he doesn't even like me anymore." Her voice shook a little, and she turned her eyes away from me to stare at the wall of hay again.

I forgot about Skeets. "That can't be true," I told her.

"What makes you think so?" She looked back at me with hope in her eyes that I could somehow convince her.

"I don't know. It just can't be. You're family, and family always likes each other," I stammered, knowing that I wasn't making a lot of sense and not at all sure that what I said was even true.

Her eyes stayed sad. "Oh, I know he still loves me like a brother, that sort of thing. But I mean we used to *like* each other so much. It was more than just ordinary brother-sister feeling. When we were afraid or lonely or sad we knew how the other one felt without having to be told in words."

She stopped talking. I didn't know what else to say to help, so I just sat there on the hay while I waited for her to go on and wondered if it would make her feel better if I held her hand.

After a long time she started talking again. "I still know how he feels. He just won't let me help him any more. He wants me to leave him alone."

"Then maybe you should." When I felt her stiffen beside me, I tried to explain. "I mean maybe he wants to do some things on his own, but he doesn't know how to tell you that straight out. So instead he's just shutting you out."

"That's silly," she said.

"Yeah, I guess so."

She leaned back against the hay beside me with a sigh. "But probably true. It's those crazy Truelanders. He wants to be one so much, and he thinks that they haven't asked him because they think he's some sort of sissy, and that they think he's a sissy because of me." She began to pluck at some of the dried up leaves on the hay. "And it probably is because of me that the Truelanders haven't asked him to join, but not because of the reason Ray thinks. Eric is just trying to get back at me through Ray."

"Get back at you? Why?"

She pulled out a handful of hay and crumbled it to shreds before letting it sift to the floor. "Because I broke off with him last year instead of waiting for him to break off with me."

"Harden's got it in for a lot of people," I said. "Maybe we should form a counter club."

"What? And have gang wars?" Shea looked at me with a little smile.

"Sometimes I think I'm in some kind of war already."

Shea's smile disappeared, and she reached over and took my hand as I'd wanted to take hers moments before and hadn't had the nerve. "If it's a war, you're going to win it."

As I stared into her eyes, I forgot all about Eric and the Truelanders, Ray and Skeets, and even bridges. I put my free hand on her cheek, and when she didn't pull away, I moved my face closer to hers.

I could have stayed there with my lips touching her lips all day, but after a moment she pulled away and jumped up. "I've got to be getting back to the house. It'll be time to take their lunches out to the barn."

I stood up, too, reluctant to leave our hidden spot.

"But first," she said, her usual smile returning. "First, I want to show you something about this barn."

I followed her through the stacks of hay. I couldn't figure out why she was acting so nervous until she threw open a small square door on the end of the barn.

Although we had entered the barn from the ground, it had been built into the side of a hill, and now we were in a loft. She sat down in the doorway, her feet dangling outside, while the air flowed in around her. I stayed back, away from the opening.

"You can get a great view of the farm from here," Shea said. "And the woods down toward the river. See, the leaves are beginning to change colors already." She paused a minute before she went on. "I love to sit here and look out. There's always a breeze even on the hottest days in the summer, and in the winter the loft full of hay seems to keep it from being so cold. I can sit here and think things out."

When I didn't make a move to join her in the opening, she glanced over her shoulder and said, "Don't you want to look out at the view?"

"I can see from here," I said.

"You can't see very much." She turned her head back to the view.

"Enough." I could see how the sky framed her on every side.

"It's not really that high," Shea said. "Ray and I used to jump out of this window sometimes when the snow was deep. It was like jumping into a big cold pillow, but once we tried it when the snow wasn't deep enough and Ray broke his collar bone."

I leaned against the hay bales and waited for her to give up. I couldn't go dangle my feet out her loft window. "Did that stop you?" I asked, just to say something.

"We never jumped much after that, but I don't know whether it was the broken bone or whether we just got older before the next winter. You know how it is. One year it's fun playing hide-and-seek, that kind of thing, and the next year those things are for kids."

"I guess so."

"Did you ever have a broken bone?" she asked too casually.

"You mean did I ever fall off a bridge or some-where high and break a bone and that's why I'm afraid to come over and sit beside you?"

She turned away from the view, leaned her back against the side of the loft door, and clasped her knees close to her chest. She looked straight at me for a moment before she said, "Yes, that's exactly what I mean."

My heart began to jerk uneasily inside me. Her perch there in the opening looked so precarious that when a puff of wind blew in and lifted her blond hair off her shoulders, I wanted to reach out and pull her back away from the sky.

"No, no broken bones." I managed to get the

words past the lump forming in my throat. "No falls except in my imagination."

"You imagine falling?" she asked.

"Only if I'm on a bridge." Or dreaming, I thought to myself, as last night's dream came vividly to mind.

She sat there and stared at me for what seemed like a long time. I couldn't see her face clearly because of the bright light that flowed in from behind her, but I didn't need to see her eyes to know she was disappointed even before she said, "You're not going to come look out, are you?"

"No."

With a little sigh, she stood up. She leaned out into the air to grab the loft door, and my heart jerked to a stop. Then it pounded with relief when she pulled the door closed with no problem.

In the truck riding the rest of the way to her house, neither one of us said much. At the house, her mother had the lunches ready for Shea to ferry back out to the barn. I helped her load everything up before I said I had to go home.

Shea didn't try to convince me to stay. She just waved goodbye before she drove the truck back across the field toward the barn.

As I walked across the hayfield toward my house, I was glad when the sun went in behind some clouds. I was tired of all that brightness. I hoped the clouds kept coming, thicker and grayer, so that I'd have an excuse to hole up in my room all afternoon. I smiled when a raindrop hit my face before I went in the backdoor.

Mom looked up from her typewriter when I came in. "There's some stuff in the fridge if you're hungry."

"Sure, Mom. I'll find something," I said.

The sporadic clatter of the typewriter followed me out to the kitchen and then up to my room. So did Abigail, and I was glad to have her company.

In my room I turned on my little television and lay down on the bed to watch the football game. Abigail curled up beside me and purred softly as I stroked her fur lightly. On the tv screen, the players moved back and forth following the ball, but though I tried, I couldn't keep my mind on the plays. Instead I kept thinking that surely I could have gone over and taken a peek out the loft window at Shea's view. Surely I could have done that much.

That night the dream came back the same as the night before. I was dangling in the air, and then I was grabbing at nothing as I fell. This time I must have cried out because when I opened my eyes Mom was in my doorway.

"Are you all right, Lucas?" she asked.

I had to wait till the blood slowed its pounding through my veins before I could answer. "Sure, Mom. It was just a dream. I'm sorry I woke you."

She came over to sit on the edge of my bed and stroke the hair back from my forehead. "You're shaking," she said.

"I'll stop in a minute." I forced my breaths out slow and even. "I'm okay."

"Of course, you are," she said softly, still stroking my head. "You used to have nightmares all the time when you were little. Do you remember?"

"Yes."

"And I'd sit with you and tell you stories about your teddy bear until you went back to sleep. I'd talk and talk taking the stories in circles and never making much sense I'm afraid. But you never would tell me about the dreams. I thought if you could talk about them it would help."

"If I still had Bill the bear, you could take him on another adventure tonight."

"He's probably around here somewhere packed away in a box."

"It doesn't matter. I'm too old for him now anyway," I said, sitting up a little.

"Yes, I suppose you are." She dropped a soft kiss on my forehead before she stood up and looked down at me. After a moment, she said, "Just remember, Lucas. Dreams are only dreams. They're not real no matter how real they seem while we're asleep."

"I know, Mom. Thanks."

After she left, I waited till she turned the hall light out and went back in her room before I eased out of bed to go stand by the window.

I stared out at the darkness. I had forgotten that I'd never told Mom about the dream. And I'd never told her about the bridges, about Dad pulling me across them, or about the awful fear. She knew I didn't like bridges, but I'd never really told her how much. I didn't want her to be ashamed of me the way Dad was.

So she couldn't understand about the dream and how, though it was a dream, there was something too real about it all as if it might have really happened. Yet I couldn't have fallen, not the way I fell in the dream.

It was a dream. Only a dream. I hadn't really fallen off a bridge. No one had dangled me over the edge in air and then turned me loose. It wasn't real.

Unless, of course, it was a dream of the future instead of the past.

I shook the thought away. I couldn't fall off of a bridge because I wasn't going out on one. No matter how many friends I lost. No matter if Shea turned her back on me, too.

I went back to my bed, punched my pillow more than necessary, and lay back down. I didn't go to sleep for a long time.

Chapter 9

The next day after lunch, I answered a knock on the door to find Shea standing there with her usual smile. I was so surprised that I blurted out, "What are you doing here?"

Her smile became a little uncertain as she answered, "I wanted to see you."

"I figured you'd given up on me," I said.

Her smile came back, wider than before. "I don't give up that easily."

I just looked at her without saying anything, and after a moment, she asked, "Well, are you going to let me come in, or are you going to slam the door in my face?"

I stepped back to let her in just as Mom came in from the kitchen.

"Shea, how nice to see you again," she said. "Lucas didn't tell me you were coming over."

"He didn't know I was coming. I sort of invited myself," Shea said with a sideways grin over at me. "I thought maybe we could go for a walk."

"I'm sure he'd love to. Lucas has been spending entirely too much time moping around the house lately by himself," Mom said, then frowned a little before she went on. "I don't know what's happened to Jacob. He used to be over here all the time." Mom looked at me. "He's not sick, is he?"

"No, Mom. Jacob's not sick. He's just been busy."

"I see. Oh well, everybody's always too busy," she said with a smile over at Shea. "But come sit down, Shea. We'll clear you off a place." Mom gathered up the Sunday paper that we'd left spread out all over the couch.

As Shea moved toward the couch, she looked around and asked, "Where's your kitten?"

"Abigail?" Mom said. "I let her out a few minutes ago."

"Then I guess if Shandy came with you, Abigail's probably up in a tree again by now," I said.

The words were barely out of my mouth when we heard Shandy barking outside and frantic scratching on the back door. When I opened the door, Abigail scooted through, her fur standing out in points and her tail looking twice as big as usual.

"I'm sorry," Shea said. "I thought I'd sneaked off without Shandy seeing me, but I guess he tracked me down."

"No permanent harm done." Mom laughed and scooped up the kitten. "I'll go feed her. That should calm her down."

"How about that walk, Luke?" Shea asked after Mom had carried Abigail out to the kitchen. "I brought some sandwiches for a picnic later." She held up her backpack.

I looked at her suspiciously. "Where are we going to have this picnic?"

"Nowhere special. Anywhere." When I still hesitated, she added, "Don't look at me like that. I haven't go anything planned. Honest."

I didn't entirely believe her, but I yelled to Mom that I was leaving and followed Shea outside.

We walked along an old country road that wound through the trees, and around every curve I expected to see a bridge where Shea could test my fear again, but the nearest thing to a bridge we came to was a concrete slab over a creek. The creek running under it was shallow and rocky, and the clear water sparkled invitingly in the sunshine.

We decided to leave the road and head up the middle of the creek stepping from rock to rock. Of course, Shandy kept plopping down in the water to cool off. Then when he stood up, he always shook himself off, spraying us with the excess water.

By the time we came to the huge flat boulder with the creek flowing all around it, we were already wet. So we just took off our shoes, splashed through the deeper water around the boulder, and climbed onto the rock. After we put the soft drinks Shea had brought along into the creek to cool, we lay back on the warm rock to let the fall sunshine dry us out.

It was a perfect place, hidden and quiet except for the sound of the creek water pushing over and around the rocks in the stream and an occasional bark from Shandy as the dog hunted rabbits in the trees along the creek.

For a while we didn't say anything, just held hands and studied the sky far above us. Then when we did begin to talk it wasn't about bridges. All afternoon, we didn't talk about bridges at all.

Later when I walked her home, I told her how much I'd enjoyed the picnic.

She smiled and squeezed my hand.

Then I was the one who almost spoiled everything by bringing up bridges. "And thanks for not talking about bridges."

Her eyes got serious. "I just thought it would be fun to have a picnic. And it was fun, wasn't it?"

"It was fun," I said.

She was still studying me with her clear blue eyes. "But you still think I might try to trick you into doing something you don't want to do."

"There's no way you could trick me out onto a bridge, Shea. No way."

"I wouldn't try," Shea said. "Honest."

I wanted to believe her, and so as the days passed, I didn't worry too much about bridges. I just enjoyed being with Shea. We sat together on the bus every morning and afternoon, and managed to find a few minutes to talk in the hall between classes.

Things at school had settled down to a weird kind of normal. The Truelanders still turned their backs on me when they saw me, but while none of the other kids actually rushed to be my best friend, they didn't avoid me either. I was just another kid who might be a little strange but I was harmless.

Now that I was one of them, I began to notice

there were quite a few of us in the halls. Kids who for some reason or other didn't quite fit in with everybody else and who didn't seem to care. I worked hard, too, at seeming not to care.

Skeets had no such worries. He was an outcast, and he wanted it that way. If anyone had offered him friendship, he'd have laughed in their face. He didn't want anyone to like him.

He hadn't forgotten me or his threat. Monday he promised to break both my arms if I didn't stay away from Shea. Tuesday he tripped me as I was going into English class. Wednesday he was mercifully absent. Thursday he threatened to push me down the stairs, and Friday he shoved me face first up against the wall, my nose trying to dig a hole in the concrete.

"Are you dumb or what, kid? I told you to stay away from Shea, and everyday I see you talking to her. That's worse than dumb, kid. It's dangerous."

"I can't stop Shea talking to me if she wants to," I managed to get out even though my mouth was mashed against the wall. "Shea does what she wants. You know that."

"Then you'd better figure out a way to make her not want to talk to you," he said. "I'd hate to have to hurt you, kid."

"I'm not afraid of you," I said.

It was such a ridiculous thing to say that I almost laughed. There I was, totally helpless and at his mercy, and yet it was true. I wasn't afraid of him. I didn't want him to hurt me, but I wasn't afraid.

With a laugh, he turned me loose. "Everybody's afraid of Skeets," he said when I turned around to look at him. "If they know what's good for them."

"Maybe so," I said calmly. The first bell had already rung, and I was going to be tardy for class. I wasn't the only one. A few kids stood around in the hall, watching us. One of them was Eric Harden.

Skeets was still glaring at me, and I went on. "Are you sure it's you I need to be afraid of, or are you just somebody else's muscle?" Deliberately I moved my eyes from Skeets to Eric Harden.

"Fear's made you soft in the head, Dillon," Skeets said. "I don't do nothing except what I want to do."

My eyes came back to him. "And I may be afraid of some things, but not of you, Joseph Skeets."

Before he could hit me, I slipped away up the hall so quickly that Eric barely had time to turn his back on me. I smiled a little as I passed him and then smiled bigger when I slipped through my classroom door a split second before the tardy bell rang because I knew Eric wouldn't have had time to make his own class.

That afternoon on the bus, Shea sat down beside me and said, "I hear you and Skeets had another go at each other in the hall today."

"I don't know what you mean by a 'go at each other.' Skeets grabs me, does whatever he wants to do, and then lets me go. There's no way I can fight against him, Shea. If I tried to hit him, it would be like committing suicide."

"Oh, Skeets wouldn't really hurt you." I looked over at her, and she went on. "Okay. Okay. I know you don't believe me about Skeets, but he's always nice to me."

"Yeah, but just because he likes you doesn't mean he likes anybody else. I think you're the one and only person he likes in the whole school."

Shea blushed. "You make it sound as if he *really* likes me."

"Maybe he does," I said thoughtfully. "That might explain a lot."

"What do you mean?"

"Oh, I don't know. Just that he doesn't like it when you talk to me. I thought Eric was putting him up to all this stuff he's doing, but maybe not. Maybe he's just jealous."

"That's crazy," Shea said, still blushing. "Skeets and I are friends. That's all."

"That may be the way you feel, but that doesn't mean it's the way he feels."

"I don't want to hear any more of this," Shea said. "It's too silly."

She sat back in the seat and stared straight ahead. I waited till the blush faded from her cheeks before I said anything else. Then I didn't mention Skeets or the other thing I wanted to know. Did Skeets have any reason to be jealous of me? Maybe Shea thought we were just friends, too, in spite of the kisses.

I wanted to be more than just friends, more than a charity case when it came to her friendship.

With my stop coming up next, she said, "Are you coming over later?"

"Sure, if you want me to. You got something planned?"

"I may have to dig potatoes."

"Sounds like fun," I said as I stood up. "I'll bet I'm good at it."

She laughed. "Mama has started calling me Tom Sawyer because of the way I rope you into all my chores."

I paused in the yard to wave goodbye to her. All week it had been the same. Every afternoon I'd gone to her house and helped her with some kind of chore. Sometimes we'd talked about bridges, but she hadn't tried to get me on one. She hadn't even suggested going back to the barn loft with me. And while I still didn't want to sit in the loft window with her, I wouldn't have minded a repeat of the kiss among the hay bales. I wondered if I could figure out a way to steal a kiss in the potato patch.

Shea was unusually quiet as we worked in her garden that afternoon. With a potato fork I lifted the potatoes out of the dirt, and Shea put them in a bucket. When the bucket was full, I carried it to the end of the row and emptied it into a gunnysack while she held the top of the sack open.

We worked well together, and I sort of enjoyed jabbing the fork into the earth to lift the big white potatoes out of the dirt. Shea laughed at me and said that was only because I'd never had to do very much of it.

"After a while, your back gets to hurting and pretty soon you're crawling around on your knees picking up the potatoes. Ray could tell you all about it. He hates to dig potatoes."

"Where is Ray today?" I asked as I pushed the fork into the ground again. "I never see him when I'm here."

Shea concentrated on the potatoes she was placing in the bucket. "Dad has him busy at one thing or another."

"Is Skeets working for your father this week, too?" I leaned down on the handle of the fork and raised the mound of dirt up until the potatoes burst out the top while I thought about the walk home through the hayfield. Every day I'd expected Skeets to be lying in wait for me. Yet I kept coming to Shea's house.

"He's here today, I think. I'm not sure what they're doing, but Dad promised Ray they'd be through early." She stared at one of the potatoes a long time before she dropped it in the bucket. Then she stared out at nothing without picking up any more of the potatoes I pitched her way.

"You tired?" I asked, leaning on my fork. "I guess we could take a break, couldn't we? We're almost finished with the row."

"I'm not tired," Shea said, but still she sat down in the dirt between the rows. "It's just Ray. And he wouldn't want me talking to you about it, but I've got to talk to somebody."

"About what?"

"He's going out with them tonight. The Truelanders," she added although I knew who she was talking about at once.

"So they finally asked him." I stuck the fork in the ground and dropped down beside Shea. "Then I guess he's happy."

"He's so excited he's almost frantic."

I picked up a clod of dirt and mashed it in my hand before I let the cool, soft dirt sift away between my fingers. "It'll be okay, Shea. They don't do anything really bad. It was me that caused the problem, not them."

"I don't like them," Shea said. "Willie, Mike, Jeremy, Jacob, none of them, and especially Eric. He's the one who's changed the Truelanders into something bad."

I wasn't about to take up for Eric Harden so I just let her keep talking.

"I mean the Truelanders have been around forever."

"Yeah, I know. Jacob told me," I said.

"But they were just a bunch of boys who like camping out, that sort of thing. Eric's turned that into some sort of secret cult. Something about that bothers me." She smoothed out a spot in the soft dirt, running her hand over the surface again and again. "I tried to get Ray to understand that. I told him that the way they'd treated you showed what kind of guys they were."

"But he wouldn't listen," I said. "He told you he wasn't a coward like me, and that whatever the Truelanders did to me was no more than a coward deserved."

She didn't look up at me, just kept smoothing her spot of dirt. "Something like that."

"Well, you don't have to worry. Ray's not afraid of heights. He was up on the barn roof, wasn't he?"

"Yeah, but he's afraid of other things. And if something happens and the Truelanders give him the kind of silent treatment they've been giving you, he couldn't bear it. I know he couldn't."

I reached over and put my hand on top hers, messing up her smooth square of dirt. "It'll be okay. Nothing will happen."

"I wish I could believe that, but I have a bad feeling." She looked away toward the trees in the distance that eventually led down to the river. "I think Eric intends for something to happen. I think that's the only reason Ray was asked to come to their camp out."

Chapter 10

It was nearly dark when I went across the hay-field back home. My heart speeded up at every shift of shadow and rustle of grass.

Some night when I came this way, Skeets was going to be waiting for me. It was only a matter of time, and while I might not fear Skeets the way I feared bridges, I didn't exactly look forward to getting beaten up by him. So I was relieved when I made it to my yard without Skeets stepping out of the shadows in front of me.

Then I saw Dad's truck in the driveway, and my relief vanished. Dad had a way of looking at me and knowing when something was wrong in a way that Mom never did. Lately Mom stayed so wrapped up in the characters she was writing about that she didn't pay much attention to anything else. It had taken her a week to notice Jacob had quit coming around.

But Dad would notice right off that things weren't the same as the last time he was home. He'd want to know what I'd done to make Jacob quit coming over and why I was jumping at my shadow. When he found out what had happened, he'd push courage at me like a dose of cough syrup.

"To grow up to be a strong man you have to learn to face your fears." I'd heard him say that a million times, and just as many times I'd failed his tests of courage.

Shea's tests hadn't been as hard, but I'd failed a few of them, too. Worse, I knew she had something new in mind to try. Although she never came right out and told me what she was planning, she kept hinting at something.

Today she'd been too worried about Ray to think much about me and bridges. She'd only brought up the reason for my fear once.

"If you could only remember why you're afraid," she'd said. "I mean if you understood it, then we'd know better what to do about it." She made it sound as if the knowledge of the beginnings of my fear would be the key to unlocking some secret store of courage inside myself.

She had talked so much about it in the last week that she had almost convinced me that it might be true. Maybe something had happened to cause me to fear bridges. I had been trying all week to remember the first time I was afraid on a bridge, but the fear was older than my memories.

As I went past Dad's truck to the backdoor, I thought if there was a reason for my fear, he would know. I hesitated a few minutes before I went inside. I couldn't ask him. Not about the bridges.

In the living room, Mom glanced up from the mystery she was reading and said, "I saved you a plate."

I looked around. "Where's Dad?"

"He was tired from the drive home, so he went to bed early." Mom shut her book, using her finger to keep her place. "He's had a hard week. A couple of the workers got hurt, and now they're short-handed."

"It's a wonder he came home then." I sat down in the chair across from the couch.

"I think he needed time away from it all. Time to come home and unwind. So we mustn't bother him with any of our problems."

"What problems?" I asked. Had she noticed more than I thought?

"Oh, I don't know. The car's making a weird noise, and the backdoor won't close right anymore. But those things can wait for another weekend."

"Yeah." I couldn't remember Dad ever fixing that kind of thing anyway, but I didn't say so.

Mom reopened her book, but when I didn't get up to go out to the kitchen, she asked, "Aren't you hungry? Did Shea's mother feed you again?"

"Just a soft drink," I said. "Shea and I dug potatoes."

Mom smiled. "Who'd have ever thought you'd like playing farmer, or is it just Shea's company you like?"

"Both, I guess." I grinned self-consciously.

"She is cute."

Mom's eyes went back to her book, and in a minute she was absorbed in the story again. The room was so quite I could hear poor Abigail out in the garage crying to be let back into the house.

"Do you think it'd be all right if I let Abigail in since Dad's asleep?" I asked.

"Not a good idea," Mom said without looking up from her book. "Your father might get up, and you know how he hates having the cat in here. She won't like it, but she'll survive in the garage till Monday."

I listened to the cat cry and wondered if I could put my problems away in a garage till Monday so that Dad wouldn't notice them. Shea said that was sort of what I was doing already, that I was shoving aside the reason for my fears so I wouldn't have to deal with it.

Dad would like Shea. No, he'd love her, especially if he knew how she kept trying to get me to face my fears.

What neither of them seemed to realize was that I didn't want to be afraid. I just was. Again I heard Shea whisper in my mind. "But there has to be a reason."

I watched Mom turning the pages of her book as she read swiftly through the story. Maybe she knew the reason behind my fears. Maybe she just acted as if she never knew I was afraid.

"Mom," I said. After a moment she looked up as though surprised to see me still there. "Can I ask you something?"

"You look so serious, Lucas."

I nodded and swallowed hard while I tried to come up with the right words for my question.

"Is it something about sex?" She sounded a little uncomfortable. "I mean you did read that book I gave you about the birds and the bees and things like that."

"It's nothing like that," I said.

Looking relieved, Mom closed her book without even checking the page number. "Then what is it?"

"The bridges."

"Bridges?" She looked puzzled. "Maybe this is

something you should ask your father. I don't know much about bridges."

"It's really more about me than bridges. I want to know why I panic when I get on a bridge. What happened to me? Did I fall once or what?"

"Panic?" Mom shook her head. "You get a little nervous, but I wouldn't say you panic."

"I would. I can't even walk out on a bridge, Mom. Surely you know that."

"Nonsense. Your father used to take you to see his bridges all the time."

"Yes. But didn't Dad ever tell you about what happened on those trips?" I asked.

"He said you couldn't see the beauty of the bridges, but then I never could either. Not like your father could anyway."

"It was more than that, Mom." I took a deep breath and plunged on. "I have an unreasonable fear of bridges. Dad thought if I kept going up on the bridges I'd get over it, but it just got worse and worse until I'd almost get paralyzed when I was on a bridge. I couldn't walk. I couldn't do anything. That's when Dad gave up on me. He thinks there's no reason for me to be afraid of being on a bridge, and I guess he's right. None of it makes any sense."

I hesitated. Mom was looking at me with a strange expression on her face as though she couldn't quite understand what I was saying. I went on. "But Shea thinks something must have happened to make me afraid of bridges and if I just knew what that was, then it might make sense. So I thought maybe if it had, you'd know something about it."

Mom frowned. "I don't remember you ever getting hurt on a bridge if that's what you mean. I'd surely know if you had whether I was there or not."

She thought a moment while her frown deepened before she shook her head and went on. "I just can't remember your father telling me about anything like that. You see, while I always went with the two of you when you were just a toddler, after that I was too glad of the time alone to work on my writing to go. I didn't get much chance in those days to work."

"What happened the times you went? Can you remember?"

"I can't remember anything out of the ordinary. Mostly I just remember how worried I'd get that you'd pull loose from me and get too close to the edge. Sometimes I'd even imagine it happening and what I'd do if it did. I worked out all kinds of elaborate schemes in my head to keep you from falling."

"But I didn't?"

"No, I carried you most of the time or made you stay right beside me."

"Was I afraid?"

"You cried if your father took you close to the edge, but I don't think you were actually afraid. At least no more than any child your age might be. Still, it bothered your father when you cried. He wanted you to like the bridges the way he did. I kept telling him you were too little, to give you time."

Time. I looked down at my hands. Time hadn't solved anything, only made things worse. It was quiet between us, and I could hear Abigail crying again.

After a few minutes, Mom broke the silence. "Everybody's afraid of something, Lucas." I looked up to see Mom's face clear of the puzzled worry of a few minutes before. "I mean I'm afraid of lightning. Your father's afraid of bees. There's nothing wrong with being afraid of something. Especially heights. Lots of people feel a little funny about heights. It's a normal enough fear."

"I guess so."

"Very common, in fact." Mom no longer seemed to be looking at me but through me at something beyond. I thought maybe she'd remembered something that might help me until she said, "You know, that might make a good story idea. One of the characters could be afraid of something and then get in a situation where he has to do that thing anyway. That would make for good conflict."

"I'm not a character in one of your stories, Mom." My hands clenched the arms of the chair.

"Of course not. That's where the imagination has to take over and make something happen." Mom began scribbling in the notebook she kept close at hand all the time.

I wanted to jerk it out of her hands. I wanted to make her look at me, make her worry about my problems and not just make those problems into a story.

After a minute, I stood up. "I guess I'll go eat," I said.

"What did you say?" Mom said vaguely, not looking up.

"I said I guessed I'd eat."

"Okay," Mom said, writing furiously across the pages of her notebook.

She'd have said okay if I'd told her I was going

out to hunt tigers—or jump off a bridge. She, no doubt, could use the idea in a story.

I stuck my plate in the microwave and slammed the door so hard that the oven rocked backwards a little.

Mom didn't understand about the bridges. She'd comforted me through countless nightmares when I was little, but she'd never known what the nightmares were about. I didn't either. I didn't know what any of it was about.

I did know I didn't like being turned into a character in a story. And I didn't like having my courage tested all the time as if I was some kind of laboratory rat. I had a weird crazy fear of bridges and that was that. There wasn't any reason. It just was.

I was going to block it all out of my mind. I could almost hear Shea telling me that was my problem now. That I'd blocked out the reason for my fear. That I wasn't a coward because I was afraid of bridges, but because I was afraid to find out why.

I'd tried to find out, I argued back in my head. I'd asked Mom.

But I hadn't asked Dad.

I took my plate out of the microwave and ate standing up. The meatloaf was too hot and the potato still cold, but I ate it anyway.

I'd never asked him before, and I couldn't ask him now. We couldn't talk about bridges. Or fear.

Up in my room, I looked out my window at the night. The huge moon hung just above the horizon and cast a shimmering light over the trees.

I thought about the Truelanders gathered in the woods, all proving their courage over and over by testing the courage of others. I wondered how Ray would do. I had no way of guessing.

All the days I'd gone over to Shea's, I'd never talked to Ray. A few times we could have talked, but Ray had been too much a Truelander even though he wasn't officially in the club. While he hadn't actually turned his back on me at the farm, he'd ignored me just the same. Maybe it had paid off for him. He was getting his chance.

I wondered if Shea was still worrying about him and knew she was. All my efforts to convince her that Ray would be all right had been useless.

I could take her to them. The full moon would give us plenty of light to make our way through the woods, and we could hide and watch them. Then she could see for herself that Ray was all right.

In the living room, Mom was still writing away in her notebook. When she heard me come in the room, she looked up. "I thought you'd gone up to bed," she said.

"Did you forget?" I said as casually as I could. "I'm going camping tonight." I waited to see if it would work. Mom did forget lots of things I told her if she was writing at the time. She'd probably forgotten already where she'd gotten the idea about fears.

"Oh. With Jacob?"

I nodded enough to please her.

"It's sort of cool tonight. Maybe you'd better take an extra blanket."

"I've got one in here." I pointed down at the sleeping bag I'd brought downstairs with me. I'd have to sleep out in Shea's hayfield again after we'd spied on the Truelanders.

Mom hesitated a minute. "Well, I suppose it's okay. I don't see why your father would mind, and it's not supposed to rain."

"I'll be back early in the morning," I promised. "Probably before Dad gets up."

She threw out a few general all-purpose warnings as I eased out the door.

A few minutes later I stashed my sleeping bag behind the rolls of hay. The shifting shadows of the trees in the moonlight didn't bother me tonight. Since no one was expecting me to go back to Shea's, I didn't have to worry about Skeets waiting for me in the hayfield.

I was halfway across the field before I thought about what I was going to say to Shea, or what I would do if she'd already gone to bed.

I didn't slow down. I knew which room was hers, and if she was asleep, I'd throw pebbles at her window the way they always did on television.

I was so busy with my thoughts that it was a few minutes before I noticed that somebody was coming across the hayfield from the other direction. I stopped in my tracks and looked around, but there was no place to hide.

I had no reason to hide anyway. I wasn't doing anything wrong, and it was probably just one of the Truelanders late for the camp out. It might even be Ray.

Then as I watched him coming straight toward me, I recognized the rolling walk long before I could see his face. It was Skeets.

He came straight toward me with Shea's dog, Shandy, right behind him, and I hoped I was having a nightmare.

111

But no, I was awake, and I wasn't going to run. Instead I pushed my feet into motion and walked to meet him. I'd told him I wasn't afraid of him. The time had come to prove it.

Chapter 11

He stopped, put his hand on Shandy's collar, and waited for me. When I could see his face in the moonlight and hear Shandy's growl, I stopped, too. We stared at each other a moment without saying a word.

Finally, he smiled a little and said, "Just the kid I was looking for."

With hardly a tremble, I answered. "Okay, now that you've found me, what do you want?"

"You know that, kid. I've been warning you all week what was going to happen." He held up a fist.

"I'm not going to fight you," I said and braced myself for the blow, but when he swung, he only tapped me softly on the chin.

I flinched back a little in spite of myself but stood my ground even after Shandy lunged toward me. Skeets spoke the dog's name, and Shandy stopped in his tracks.

"I'm still not going to fight you," I repeated.

Skeets laughed. "But I might hit you harder next time."

"You might." I kept my eyes on his face, trying to ignore the growling dog.

He laughed again. "Maybe Harden's got you all wrong, Dillon," he said. "Maybe you're not such a coward after all."

"Maybe," I said.

"You can relax, kid," Skeets said after a moment. "I'm not going to beat you up tonight."

Shandy, hearing the change in his voice, stopped growling and romped off across the field.

"Then why'd you come looking for me?" I felt shakier now that I knew he wasn't going to hit me than I had a moment before when I'd thought he was.

"Shea thinks you can find them. That you don't get lost in the woods." He looked at me doubtfully.

"You mean find the Truelanders?"

"Truelanders, Blueclubbers, whatever," Skeets said and spat on the ground. "Harden's bunch."

"I can find them," I said. "I was just going over to Shea's house to see if she wanted to go with me. I thought if she could see them she'd know she didn't have anything worry about."

"It's not a game of hide-and-seek to her," Skeets said as he turned and began walking back toward Shea's house. "She says something's wrong with Ray."

I fell in beside him. It was the first time we'd ever walked side by side. He was usually a menacing step behind me. "They will barely have had time to set up camp. Ray can't be in trouble yet."

"If Shea says he is, then he is," Skeet said flatly without looking at me.

"What do you mean?" I stared at the side of his

114

face so intently that I almost stepped in a ground hog hole.

"Watch out, kid," Skeets growled as I stumbled against him. "Don't expect me to carry you home if you break your leg."

"Sorry," I mumbled, catching myself and jerking away from him.

He muttered under his breath to himself. "He can't even walk across a field without falling down, and she thinks he's some kind of army scout."

"I can do it," I said quietly. "But you didn't tell me how Shea found out something was wrong with Ray."

"I didn't say she found out. I said she knew. It's some kind of mind thing she has with Ray."

"What does she think has happened?"

"She doesn't know what, just that something has."

"Do you think something's happened?" I asked.

"It don't matter what I think. If Shea says so, that's good enough for me."

"You like Shea a lot, don't you?"

"I don't like nobody." His voice was a growl again. "Especially snot-nosed kids who ask questions."

I backed off a step or two and kept quiet until we saw Shea's house. Then when there were no lights on in any of the windows, I couldn't keep from asking one more question. "Are Shea's parents already out looking?"

"I don't see what Shea sees in you," Skeets said. "You've got to be the dumbest kid who ever lived." He went on, slowly drawing out his words so I'd be sure to understand. "This ain't the kind

115

ou tell your folks. It's the kind of thing
e care of yourself."

Shea was waiting for us out behind the garage.
"That didn't take long," she whispered.

"I met Ranger Rick on his way over here,"
Skeets said.

"Really?" When Shea looked from Skeets to
me, her face and hair shone in the moonlight.
"How come?" she asked.

"I don't know," I answered. "I just got to thinking about it and figured maybe you'd feel better
about the whole thing if you saw for yourself that
Ray was okay and that there's not that much to
any of the stuff they do."

"If there ain't nothing to it, how come you ain't
one of them then, Dillon?" Skeets asked.

"You've heard the stories," I said, and then tried
to get the right tone of sarcasm in my voice as I
went on. "Because I'm a coward."

"That's not true." Shea came hotly to my de-
fense even though she was defending me from myself. Then she said more softly, "And it's not true
about tonight either. Something's wrong. I know it
is."

"Then we'd better quit wasting time talking and
let Ranger Rick here lead us through the woods."
Skeets looked at me and added, "I'll kill you,
Dillon, if they have to send out a search party for
us in the morning."

"We won't get lost," I said. "But if you don't
want them to see us, Shea, you'd better wear a
scarf or something over your hair."

She'd come prepared, and stuck her hair up
under a black baseball cap. "You think we should
black our faces?" she asked.

Skeets made a sound between a laugh and a snort. "You two can rub mud on your faces if you want to, but it they spot me, they're the ones who'd better be worried."

They followed me through the woods, Shea behind me and Skeets behind her. Shandy came with us, but Skeets made the dog walk by his side. The only time we talked was when Shea would ask me if we were getting close, but it was a long way through the woods. Behind us I could hear Skeets muttering something about Ranger Rick and search parties. I tried not to hear exactly what he was saying.

I walked in a circle once, but when neither of them seemed to notice, I didn't point it out. Although the moonlight made the woods look different, I had no worry that I'd eventually find the Truelanders.

When I showed Skeets and Shea the outlines of the old camp, Skeets quit grumbling under his breath. We moved slowly now, stopping every few minutes to listen, but there was nothing to hear except a peculiar stillness that made us feel we were the only people in the woods, maybe in the world. Yet the Truelanders were there somewhere.

Fifteen minutes later we found Ray's sleeping bag. No one else's. Just his. They'd all been there. The grass was trampled down, and a little firewood had been gathered. But now there was nothing but Ray's sleeping bag.

"I knew something was wrong." Shea's words hung in the ghostly shimmering moonlight.

"But what?" I finally asked.

"They've done something with him, and now

117

they've all run away. Maybe he fell off the bridge." Her voice dissolved in tears.

I wanted to reach out and comfort her, but the very mention of Ray falling off the bridge woke the panic inside me.

Shandy pushed up against Shea's legs, and Skeets, his voice gentle, said, "That's crazy talk, Shea." He put his arm around her, and she leaned against his shoulder. "We'll find him. Don't you worry."

When he glanced up at me, his voice hardened. "Ranger Rick here found his sleeping bag. He can find Ray."

I still stood frozen. The trees around me wavered and disappeared to be replaced in my mind by the image of the bridge. Someone was falling, and even though I wasn't asleep, the nightmare seized my mind. I became the one falling through the whistling air.

Shandy lifted his head and growled softly at a noise in the trees behind us. Shea said, "Listen. Maybe that's Ray."

When she started to run toward the noise, it broke the lock the fear of the bridge had over my mind, and I grabbed her arm. "Wait. It might be the Truelanders coming back."

"So? What if it is?" Skeets said.

"Then maybe we'd better wait and see what they're up to. Besides if Ray's not in trouble, he won't be very happy to see us here." Before Shea could protest, I went on. "And if he is in trouble, we might find out better how to help him by eavesdropping on their plans than by confronting them face to face."

"I'm not afraid of them," Skeets said.

"I know, Skeets," Shea said. "But maybe Luke's right. Let's wait and see what's going on first."

Skeets grabbed Shandy's collar and we melted back into the shadows of the trees to wait. Whoever or whatever was coming through the woods toward the little clearing under the trees was moving very slowly, stopping every few steps before beginning to move again.

In our hiding place I barely breathed so that I could hear better. Even Shandy crouched quietly, no longer growling. But there was nothing to hear except the rustle of the brush. I had about decided it had to be Ray by himself when the sound began getting farther away instead of closer.

Shea clutched my arm and whispered, "He's going away."

"Stay here," I whispered back. "I'll catch him and bring him back."

"I'll go with you," Skeets said. He didn't seem to be able to whisper, and his voice sounded loud in the quiet of the woods.

"You'd better stay here with Shea in case . . ." I started and stopped. I didn't know what I expected to happen, but I didn't want Shea to be alone in the woods. "Well, just in case."

Without waiting for an answer, I slipped away through the trees. I had no trouble catching up with him since he was moving so slowly, and when I could see him up in front of me, I broke into a run. At the last moment he heard me closing in on him and whirled to face me.

"Jacob?" I said.

He stared back at me, as surprised to see me as I was him. "Luke, what are you doing out here?" he asked when he could find his voice.

"Looking for the Truelanders. Where's the rest of them?"

"I don't know," Jacob said. "Home, I guess. I don't really care."

"What's wrong? Did they start turning their backs on you, too?"

"I never wanted to do that, Luke, and you know it, but I thought I had to be a Truelander."

"And you are one. So you know what's going on here tonight." I kept my eyes on his face. "Where's Ray? What did you guys do to him?"

Jacob rubbed his hand across his eyes and sank back against a tree as though he was suddenly too tired to stand up. "That's the reason I came back. To try to find him, but I keep getting lost."

"What do you mean find him?"

"They left him out there, you know the way they did us, to find his way back to camp. But then when we got back to the camp out site, Eric told us to gather up our stuff, that we were going to clear out. He laughed and said we'd come back and get Ray in the morning." Jacob stopped talking and looked down at his feet.

I watched him without saying anything, and after a minute, he went on. "Eric said we didn't need any more Truelanders. He'd decided thirteen was just the right number of members."

"Then why did he ask Ray to come tonight?"

Jacob looked miserable as he answered, "Just for a joke, I guess. It was all Eric's idea."

"Some joke," I said.

"Yeah," Jacob agreed.

I looked at him a minute before I said, "Why didn't you just tell Eric the whole idea stunk and that you were going to stay here and wait for Ray instead of leaving and then sneaking back?"

"That's what you'd have done, isn't it?" Jacob said. He didn't wait for me to answer. "But I'm not as brave as you are, Luke."

"Me, brave? Now who's joking?" I turned away from him and started back through the trees. "Come on. Shea's back there at your campsite waiting for me."

When we came out of the trees into the small clearing again, Shea and Skeets had come out of hiding and were sitting on Ray's sleeping bag. Shandy raised his head up out of Shea's lap and growled, and Skeets jumped up to face us, a tree branch in his hand.

"It's okay, Skeets. It's me," I said.

"Skeets?" Jacob echoed.

"Is that you, Ray?" Shea stood up and took a step toward us, then sank back down on the sleeping bag when she recognized Jacob.

When I finished telling them what Jacob had told me about Ray, Shea looked ready to cry again. "Was he very scared when you left him out there?" she asked Jacob.

"He tried not to show it, but he was scared. I could feel him shaking when I untied his blindfold."

"Blindfold?" Skeets said. "You guys have got serious problems."

"It's one of the ways they test you," I said. "They blindfold you and take you out in the woods to see if you can find your way back."

"All that proves is how stupid you are," Skeets said.

"If you can't find your way around the woods,

then you can't be a Truelander," Jacob said, looking over at Skeets uneasily. I could tell he still hadn't figured out what Skeets was doing there.

"Who'd want to be?" Skeets said. "So I guess we can figure Ray's good and lost."

"Most everybody gets lost, or so the others told me. But they just wander around till they spot the campfire or smell the smoke from it and then find the camp that way. Of course Luke found the camp when they tested us."

"We're wasting time. If Ray's lost, we need to find Ray," I said.

"He's not just lost," Shea said. "He's hurt or something. Maybe he fell over a cliff in the dark."

"It's not that dark, Shea. He'll be all right," I said softly.

"No, Luke. I know. He's hurt."

She sounded so serious that I couldn't doubt her. Skeets must have felt the same way because he said, "Shea, you and what's-his-name here better go get help while me and Ranger Rick look for Ray."

"Maybe we could just find him ourselves," Jacob said. "I mean without calling in a bunch of other people."

"Still trying to save your hide with Harden?" I asked. "You can go on home after you take Shea to her house. That way none of the Truelanders will know you came back to look for Ray."

Jacob started to say something, but Skeets broke in on him. "You go get help," he ordered, pointing to Jacob and Shea. "We'll start searching."

I headed Jacob and Shea in the right direction and watched them disappear in the shadowy moonlight. Then I turned back to Skeets. We were alone except for Shandy who hadn't budged from his side even though Skeets had told the dog go with Shea.

Both of them were glaring at me, and I shifted uneasily on my feet. The night silence of the woods was broken only by a slight breeze rustling through the treetops.

"You scared, kid?" Skeets asked after a minute.

"What's to be scared of?" I said, trying not to think of all the ways he could answer that.

"You tell me," he said.

Something in his voice made me realize he wasn't feeling particularly brave himself and that made me feel better.

We arranged a set of signals and then split up so we could search twice as much ground. One whistle if we got lost, two if we found Ray, and three if we needed help ourselves.

As I walked away from the clearing in the opposite direction from Skeets, I thought how strange it would be to whistle for help from Skeets.

It was crazy anyway—the two of us poking around in the trees and bushes as if we expected to stumble over Ray in the dark. But I kept walking through the trees, calling out Ray's name occasionally though I wasn't sure he'd answer even if he did hear me. He'd still be trying to find the Truelanders' camp in order to pass their test. He'd have no way of knowing that it had all been a joke. Even if Shea was right and Ray was hurt and needed help, he wouldn't welcome that help from me.

I had just come out of the trees to see the river below me when the whistle pierced the night air.

Two more whistles followed the first. The signal for help.

I looked toward the sound and saw the bridge stretching across the river in the distance. My blood froze. Then the three whistles came again.

I forced myself to turn in the direction of the bridge. Hardly a minute passed until the whistles sounded again, and I made myself walk faster. There was no reason to think the bridge had anything to do with Skeets needing help.

I repeated that over and over to myself as I pushed along the rocky cliff edge following the sound of the whistles that came now with barely a pause between the sets of three.

The steep cliff side forced me back up into the woods to find an easier path. No sooner had I gone back up into the trees than Shandy bounded out in front of me, barking until my ears echoed the sound and I could no longer hear the whistles.

"Easy, boy," I edged forward. "This is no time to attack."

After a minute of frantic barking, Shandy whirled and raced off through the trees. I had no more than pulled in a relieved breath of air than the dog was back in front of me, barking again, but this time he didn't bark long before he took off back through the trees again.

I followed him. When he led me out of the trees, the bridge was directly in front of me. I felt sick as I watched Shandy run out on the railroad track to where Skeets crouched on the bridge about twenty feet from the edge. He paid the dog little mind as he put his fingers in his mouth and whistled sharply three times.

Shandy whined, shoved against him with his

nose, and then bounded back off the bridge to bark at me where I stood well back from the point where the track left the cliff and shot out into the air.

Skeets saw me then. "Don't just stand there, kid. Help me," he said. "My foot's hung."

Chapter 12

I couldn't move. I could only stare at Skeets on the bridge and think that the joke hadn't been on Ray after all. The joke had been on me.

All of it had been only a trick to get me out on the bridge. Shea must have planned it and somehow gotten them to go along with it. All of it had been an act. Ray probably wasn't even in the woods, or if he was, he was hiding back in the trees watching along with Shea and Jacob. None of it was true, and I'd fallen for the whole thing.

"Dillon!" Skeets yelled. "Get out here."

Skeets was a better actor that I would have thought he could be. He had just the right edge of panic to his voice, and the way he was spraddled on the bridge with his leg in a strange angle to the rest of his body, it looked as if he were really trapped. Even Shandy was playing along, coming through the woods to fetch me and now barking like crazy whenever Skeets quit talking.

"You might as well give up, Skeets, and come on off the bridge," I said. "I'm not coming out there."

"Give up?" His voice was hardly more than a

squeak. "I don't know what you're talking about, Dillon, but you've got to come out here and help me get my foot loose."

"Sorry. I'm afraid you'll just have to pull yourself loose." I started to turn away.

"For God's sake, Dillon, a train's going to come. You've got to help me." He hesitated, then begged, "Please."

Something about that last word stopped me. I couldn't believe Skeets would beg even for Shea. Turning back around, I stared at him.

His voice was low, intense. "I know I haven't been exactly nice to you, kid, but you don't want to watch a train splatter me all over the valley, do you?"

"There's no train. This is all just a trick to get me out onto the bridge. Shea's making you do it."

"Shea? What are you talking about?" he screamed. He stopped, took a breath, and got himself under control. "I don't know what your problem is, Dillon, but I never pegged you as mean. Me, I'm mean, but I'd help you if you were stuck out here."

"You're not stuck. You can pull your foot loose."

"I can't."

"Why not?"

"I must have broken something. I came out here to see if I could maybe spot Ray, and my boot slipped." He took his eyes off me for a second and yanked at his foot. "I've tried to pull it loose, but I can't. And a train's coming." The last word was almost a whimper.

"No train's coming."

He put his hand on the metal rail, and even from where I was standing, I could see the tremble run through him. "It's coming. I feel it." When I still didn't move, he said, "If you won't believe me, believe the dog. Just look at him."

Shandy was racing onto the bridge to sniff at him and then coming back toward me before streaking back to him. The dog was as close to frantic as I'd ever seen anything. I still wasn't sure it wasn't a trick, but I began to believe that if it was, the trick had backfired on Skeets. He couldn't get off the bridge by himself.

"I can't come out on that bridge," I said.

"I'm going to die if you don't," Skeets said quietly, all the panic draining from his voice. "I'm going to die."

I stooped down and put my hand on the railroad track. The metal did seem to vibrate, but I didn't know if that meant a train was coming. Then I heard the train whistle wafting through the night over the trees.

Skeets made a strange noise and began to jerk frantically on his leg while Shandy grabbed his jacket in his teeth and began tugging on him.

I don't know how I got on the bridge, but suddenly I was beside Skeets, turning his leg, yanking at his foot, maneuvering it through the crack in the tracks while I tried to keep from feeling the air pushing all around me. The track was thumping through the soles of my shoes now. I shut it all out as I pulled on his foot.

At last his foot jerked free of his boot, and the boot fell away from the bridge down through the air toward the water below.

As I watched the boot fall, I could hear Skeets screaming at me from somewhere far away and the steady rush of the train coming through the night, but I couldn't move. I was a little boy again, suspended in the air with nothing to grab hold of, watching my shoe slip off my foot to fall and fall and fall until finally it hit the water with a faint plop.

I didn't scream. I just watched the water far below swallow my shoe and knew that it would swallow me the same way. But then my father was lifting me back up on the bridge and saying, "See, son, I told you there was nothing to be afraid of. I wouldn't let you fall, and my bridges won't let you fall either."

The railroad bridge was shaking under my feet. My nightmare was coming true. The air was all around me, and there was nothing I could do except fall.

Something grabbed me around the middle and half carried and half dragged me along the tracks toward the end of the bridge. The train whistle pierced the air as it sounded again and again. At the last second, I was shoved off the track but the rocky ground was there to catch me.

The train's whistle sounded once more as the train pounded past filling the night with its noise and jerking me away from my waking nightmare at last.

Skeets was lying half on top of me, and without quite realizing what I was doing, I slammed my fist into his face. I hit him once, twice, and then again, but it wasn't Skeets I was seeing in my mind. It was my father.

I kept trying to hit him as the train rushed past us until he grabbed my arms and pinned me against the ground.

"Easy, kid," Skeets said when the train was at last past us and there was room for other noises besides the train. "I've already got a broken ankle. I don't need my nose broken, too."

I went limp.

He turned me loose and sat back on the ground, wincing when he moved his leg. He stared after the train. "That was close," he said.

I sat up and stared at the bridge in the moonlight while my heart did crazy dances in my chest. I couldn't say anything. I felt raw as though I'd been turned inside out and all my tender flesh was exposed to the air.

Shandy crept close to Skeets and began licking his face, and Skeets ruffled the dog's ears.

We sat there for a long time, neither of us saying anything as we stared at the bridge. Now that the train had gone, the silence was deeper than ever, but it was a good silence. We were still alive to hear it.

As if we both realized that at the same time, we turned to look at one another and say, "Thanks."

We stopped uneasily. After a minute I went on. "Look, I'm sorry about hitting you, Skeets. I don't know what came over me."

"That's okay, kid. You didn't hurt me. Nobody's ever shown you how to throw a punch." He rubbed his chin. "It was just that you took me by surprise. I didn't expect you to beat me up for pulling you off the bridge."

"I didn't expect to be on a bridge." I hesitated

a second before adding, "I'd appreciate it if you didn't tell Shea."

"Tell her what?" Skeets looked over at me. "That you threw some punches at me? She won't care about that. She'll like it."

"No, I mean about going out on the bridge." I met his eyes for a second and then looked down at the ground. Picking up a rock, I began scratching out a little hole in the dirt. "She didn't tell you to go out on the bridge and try to get me to follow you, did she?"

"Why would she do that?" Skeets said.

"I don't know."

"The night air must be affecting your brain, Dillon. I wouldn't play chicken with a train for nobody."

"I guess not." I kept digging in the ground with my rock. "But I'd really appreciate it if you didn't tell her about it anyway."

"Why?"

"She'd think I could do it again. Go out on a bridge, I mean." I looked up and threw the rock toward the bridge. "And I couldn't. I couldn't even get off that one."

"What is it with you and bridges, Dillon?"

"I'm just scared of them." Just staring at the bridge kept a chill inside me. I glanced over at Skeets. "The way you're scared of snakes."

"Snakes don't bother me. I kill them."

"I can't kill bridges."

"I guess not." Skeets slowly inched off his sock and began gingerly feeling his ankle and leg.

"Can you walk on it?" I asked.

"I got off the bridge, didn't I?"

"And came back to get me," I said.

"Don't make me no hero," Skeets said. "I was just paying you back for getting my foot loose."

"We're even then."

"Even." Skeets pushed against the ground and tried to stand up. "Give me a hand."

After I helped him to his feet, he leaned against me and tried to put weight on his foot. He didn't say a word, but I felt him wince. "You can't walk on that," I said. "I'll have to go get help."

"What about Ray?"

"Ray?" I had forgotten about Ray. "Do you think he's really out here somewhere?"

"If Shea says he is, he is, and Shea and that other kid have done gone for help. You need to find Ray."

"Okay." I looked around at the trees. "Where had you looked before the bridge?"

"In the trees, kid. I don't know. All trees look alike." He propped his hand on the dog's back and lowered himself to the ground again. "That's why I decided to try to get a better look from the bridge."

"Did you see anything?" I asked.

"Just more trees. Course if you think you can see better than me, you're welcome to look." Skeets pointed at the bridge.

Ignoring him, I looked at the dog. "Do you think you could get Shandy to go with me? He found me. Maybe he could track Ray down."

"Sure, why not?" Skeets pushed the dog away from his side and said, "Go with Dillon."

Shandy just wagged his tail and scooted back closer to Skeets.

"You go on," Skeets told me. "He'll come."

I was in the trees away from the bridge before the dog came sidling up beside me. He didn't look happy about it, but he was there. I reached down to pat his head, and he endured my touch with a low warning growl before he moved out ahead of me.

I followed along behind the dog, not paying much attention to where I was going. I still felt shaky inside.

Everything about the night seemed unreal. Me going on the bridge to help Skeets. Him pulling me out of the way of the train. Ray being lost in the woods and Jacob coming back to find him. Shandy walking along beside me. My nightmare that once upon a time had nearly happened. Last of all, me hitting Skeets.

So I moved through the woods as though I was walking through a dream, and somehow I stumbled across Ray. He was wandering through the trees, a bewildered look on his face. He looked even more confused when Shandy bounded up to him and then he saw me.

"Are you hurt?" I asked.

"What are you doing out here?"

"Looking for you," I said. "Shea thought you might be hurt."

"Shea?" He tried to peer around me. "Where is she?"

"She's gone to get help."

"Help?" He shook his head and then groaned. "I don't know what's going on."

"Are you all right?"

"My head hurts. I must have hit it on something." He touched the back of his head and then looked at me. "Do you know why I'm out here in the woods?"

"You were camping with the Truelanders. Don't you remember?"

"The Truelanders. Where are they?"

"I think they went home," I said vaguely.

"Then why am I still here?"

"I guess you got lost. Come on. Skeets is back at the bridge waiting for us."

We hadn't gone more than a dozen steps until I looked back to see Ray wandering away from me. When I stopped him, the bewildered look was back on his face. "Where am I?" he asked.

I explained it all again, but five minutes later he was just as confused as before.

I was almost glad when we came out of the trees and could see the bridge leaping across the river to the other side and Skeets sitting where I'd left him. With my hand on Ray's arm I led him over to Skeets.

"He must have a concussion," I told Skeets.

"Do you want me to go across the bridge now?" Ray said, moving that way. "Is that why we're here?"

"No." The word exploded from me, and Skeets laughed as I almost knocked Ray to the ground to stop him.

"Just not your night, is it, kid?" Skeets said.

"Or yours either." I kept one eye on Ray. If he made a break for the bridge I wanted to catch him a long time before he got there. "You'll be on crutches for a while with that ankle."

"Crutches? Joseph Skeets on crutches? No way."

"Your bones break the same as anybody else's."

"Then I guess I'll have to give up school. I can't go to school on crutches."

"Why not? Kids do it all the time."

"Football players and cheerleaders maybe, not Joseph Skeets."

"Where am I?" Ray said suddenly. He stared at Skeets and me. "What are you two doing here?"

I explained again about the Truelanders and about him getting lost.

"My head hurts." Ray leaned his head over in his hands for a few minutes. When he looked up again, he was frowning. "Then where are Eric and the others?"

Before I could think of an answer that might not upset Ray, Skeets spoke up. "They're not here. They went home."

"Went home? But you just said I was camping out with them." Ray rubbed his forehead. "I can't remember anything about tonight."

"They were playing games with you, Ray. They left you out here alone and went home," Skeets said harshly.

Ray looked at me and jumped to his feet. "They think I'm a coward like you. I'll show them. I'll prove I'm not afraid."

I tried to grab him, but Shandy must have felt the tension in the air because he growled and hurled himself at me. I fell back on the ground, Shandy's teeth glistening inches from my face.

By the time Skeets called the dog off me, Ray was stepping out on the bridge. "I'm not a coward," he yelled. His voice echoed in the night.

Skeets took one look at me and tried to get up,

but his ankle would no longer hold his weight. He groaned as he sank back down to the ground. "He'll come back," he said after a moment. "He won't fall."

Chapter 13

Out on the bridge, Ray stopped, put his hand on his head, and swayed unsteadily even as Skeets spoke.

"I'll have to go after him," I said in spite of the fact that my feet were rooted to the ground.

"You can do it, kid," Skeets said softly. "Just like me killing snakes. Every step you take kills a bridge."

I stared at the bridge hanging there in the air waiting for me. I couldn't do it, but I had to. Any second Ray might stumble. He might fall.

I forced my left foot out on the bridge. One dead bridge, I whispered to myself.

There were no side rails to cling to, only the tracks laid out on the deck of the bridge. There was nothing to hold me away from the air. A few steps in front of me, Ray leaned against some kind of signal post which stuck up from the bed of the bridge like a lonely sentinel.

"Get away from the edge," I tried to yell, but my voice came out as little more than a whisper that was lost in the air long before Ray could hear.

Yet he must have heard something, for he looked up at me, his face blank. He'd forgotten why he was there.

I pushed my right foot forward and wished I could forget I was there on the bridge with the air surrounding me, pushing me and pulling me over to the side. I slung my arms around to get free of its pull, but the air only whispered a little laugh before it wrapped around me again.

I locked my eyes on Ray's face and took two more steps, then another until I could finally reach out and touch him.

"Where am I?" he said when I grasped his wrist. "What are you doing here?"

"We're on the bridge." At the words, my mind seemed to fly apart. I hung on to enough pieces to keep my voice calm and add, "We've got to go back and help Skeets. He broke his ankle."

Ray frowned. "Skeets broke his ankle? Then we'd better help him."

"Yes." My legs were stiffening under me. I wasn't going to be able to move. I would be stuck on that bridge until the air pushed me over the edge or someone carried me off.

Ray took a step and stopped. "I guess you'd better go first. I keep forgetting. Now why are we on the bridge?"

"We're killing snakes," I said softly. Then with an iron grip on his wrist, I began moving back toward the cliff side. With each step, I imagined a bridge somewhere crumbling and collapsing. I was killing bridges, and inside me something broke a little freer with each one that fell.

I didn't see the others coming from the woods toward us until we stepped off the bridge back on solid ground and Shea came running to Ray. "Are you okay, Ray?"

Ray asked one of his favorite questions. "What are you doing here?"

"I think he must have fallen and hit his head," I said, gladly turning Ray over to her. If he ran back out on the bridge, someone else could go after him.

Shea looked over at me. "How about you, Luke? Are you okay?"

"I'm okay," I said.

My voice must have sounded sure enough to convince her because she began shepherding Ray back to where her father and someone else were bent over Skeets. I eased off across the railroad tracks in the other direction, slid behind the closest tree, and leaned there while the tremble shook loose every muscle in my body.

A hand came down on my shoulder. "I saw you out there on the bridge, Luke."

"Dad." As I whirled to face my father, all I could think of was how I'd pounded my fists into Skeets while in my mind I'd seen my father. I dropped my eyes to the ground and managed to ask Ray's question. "What are you doing here?"

"Shea's father called me and said you were out here."

I could feel Dad's eyes boring into me. I tried to shop shaking, but I couldn't. Even worse, I was afraid I was going to be sick.

"I saw you out on the bridge," Dad said again. "I knew you could do it."

"I couldn't do it again," I said.

"Of course you could if you wanted to," Dad said.

"I don't want to. I didn't want to then. I never wanted to." My voice rose. I clenched my fists and forced myself to quit yelling. "You made me."

"I was just trying to help you, Lucas. I didn't want you to be afraid."

"But I was afraid. I still am." I didn't look over my shoulder at the bridge behind me, but I felt it there. "I'll always be afraid."

In the strained silence that followed my words I could hear the others talking to Ray and Skeets. Dad's voice, when he finally spoke, was soft, thoughtful. "I never could understand why you were afraid of being on a bridge."

"You. You made me afraid of bridges." Again my voice rose as I remembered dangling in the air, my shoe falling.

"Me? No, son. I did everything I could to keep you from being afraid and to help you get over your fear. More likely it was the way your mother used to hang on to you every time we went out on a bridge."

I shook my head, but I couldn't say anything.

Dad went on. "None of that matters now. The important thing is that you overcame your fear when you had to."

"No, Dad. I'm still afraid."

"Maybe," Dad said, his eyes intent on me. "But you overcame your fear enough to do what you had to do. That showed courage and I'm proud of you."

Courage? I could hardly believe my ears. Dad couldn't be telling me I had courage. I began to wonder if I was dreaming again.

"Dillon!" Skeets yelled from the other side of the railroad tracks. "Get over here and help me."

I began walking back toward the others, glad I didn't have to say anything else to Dad right then. I had to have time to think everything through.

Dad followed me, and when Skeets yelled at me again, Dad said, "Who is that?"

"That? Oh, that's just Skeets. He's friends with Shea, and he was helping us look for Ray. I think he broke his ankle."

"He needs to learn a nicer way to ask for help."

"That was nice," I said. "For Skeets."

Skeets leaned on me and my father, and Mr. Ashburn led Ray. Shea fluttered back and forth between us, not sure who needed her the most.

On one of her trips back to see about Skeets, she told me that Jacob was waiting at the road with the cars. "He didn't go home, Luke," she said.

I muttered some kind of answer, but I didn't say too much. I was afraid she'd say something about the bridge, and I didn't want to talk about the bridge or the Truelanders or any of it there in front of Dad.

Besides, I didn't have much breath left over for talking. It was a long way through the woods, and Skeets leaned heavily on me as he half hopped and half walked. Although he never said a word about his ankle hurting, I could feel the shudder run through him each time he touched that foot to the ground.

Dad must have felt it, too, because he said, "I can try carrying you piggyback, Skeets."

"It ain't that bad," Skeets said quickly. "It just crunches a little every once in a while, but I can make it."

As the trees went on and on, I had plenty of time to think about what Dad had said about me overcoming my fear to go out on the bridge. The first time with Skeets, the thought of the train had pushed me and I hadn't even realized I was going out on the bridge, but the second time there had been no train. There had been only the need to get Ray off the bridge, and somehow, I'd done it.

I had conquered my fear at least for a few minutes. So what if I was sick afterwards. I had done it, and that was the important thing.

Even with Skeets leaning on me, I began to feel lighter as though I had shed an extra heavy coat back at the bridge. I didn't want to ever walk out on another bridge, but at least now I knew I could. And with that knowledge, I knew it didn't matter what anybody else thought now. I knew I wasn't a coward.

I guess Skeets was doing some thinking of his own as we made our way through the endless trees, because when we stopped once to catch our breath, he said, "Hey, kid, I'm sorry about all that school business and the other stuff." He looked up to be sure Shea wasn't close enough to overhear before he went on. "I guess I didn't like you getting so friendly with Shea."

"I thought maybe Harden had put you up to it," I said.

"Harden? I wouldn't do anything for that bum," Skeets said. "Anyway, I'm not very good at stuff like this, but if it helps anything you can tell the kids at school that you gave me a black eye. That ought to make them leave you alone."

"Did I give you a black eye?" I peered up at his face in the moonlight.

"It's a little puffy. Nothing serious." Skeets put his arm around my shoulders again as we prepared to start off again. "I guess you throw a better punch than I thought."

"Were you two fighting?" Dad's voice was sharp.

"Not enough to hurt," Skeets said. He tried a laugh that came out as more of a gasp as we started moving again.

On the other side of Skeets, I could almost hear Dad waiting for me to explain what Skeets was talking about, but I couldn't tell Dad about hitting Skeets.

I was relieved when we spotted the car's headlights through the trees ahead of us since that meant there would be no time for talking. Dad loaded Skeets in the back seat of our car while Shea and her family climbed into their car. Jacob and I got in the front with Dad, but nobody said much. Dad took Jacob home and then dropped me off at the house before heading on to the hospital with Skeets.

The next morning Dad told me the doctor at the emergency room had put a cast on Skeets's leg and sent him home on crutches, but they'd kept Ray overnight for observation.

"It looked like Skeets was going to have a pretty good shiner," Dad said. We were eating breakfast, and Dad looked at me over his coffee cup.

I ducked my head away from his eyes. "It was all pretty crazy out there about that time. I didn't know what I was doing." I shoved the last of my eggs and toast in my mouth to keep from having to say anything else. I couldn't explain it to Dad. It was enough that I was beginning to understand myself.

I didn't try to explain it to Shea either when she came over later to go with me to get Ray's sleeping bag out of the woods. Skeets had told her all about the train and his foot being caught and what I'd done for him and what he'd done for me. He even told her about me hitting him.

"Skeets told you all that?" I said when she'd finished.

"Yeah, pretty amazing, isn't it? Now I want to hear your version," she said as we walked through the trees that looked different in the sunlight.

"It's the way Skeets said." I stared straight ahead. "It's just that after the bridge I had to hit somebody and Skeets happened to be the only person handy. It's a wonder he didn't kill me."

"No, he likes you." Shea looked at me thoughtfully. "And Skeets doesn't like very many people."

"Yeah. There's nothing like beating up somebody and having them beat up you in return to make people chummy."

Shea smiled a little. "I can see you don't want to talk about what happened on the bridge, but it's okay now, isn't it? You're not afraid anymore, are you?"

I looked at her and laughed. "You know, when I first saw Skeets out there on the bridge, I thought you'd planned it all just to trick me into going out on a bridge."

"I wouldn't do that, Luke." When I just looked

at her, she laughed a little and went on. "Well, nothing quite that drastic anyway, but even if I didn't plan it, you have to admit that it worked."

"No, I still get shaky just thinking about bridges, but at least now I know I'm not a coward."

"I always knew you weren't a coward, Luke," she said softly. "I just never realized how brave you were until last night." Then instead of me kissing her, she kissed me.

After the kiss, we walked on through the trees, holding hands and not saying much. We didn't seem to need words.

Monday morning on the bus, Shea told me Ray had come home and was doing all right. "He still doesn't remember what happened, but maybe that's just as well. Thank goodness he's decided the Truelanders aren't such a great bunch after all."

"I guess Jacob decided that, too. He came over yesterday to shoot some baskets," I said.

"Then you're friends again."

"I doubt if we can ever be friends the way we used to be. Too much has happened." I glanced over at her. "Besides, I've got other friends now."

Shea grinned and let me take her hand. "Everything worked out okay after all, didn't it?"

"Except for Skeets," I said. "He said he wouldn't come back to school if he had to come on crutches."

"We'll make him come."

And somehow she did. On Thursday morning Skeets showed up at school, and Shea and I made up a schedule so that one of us could carry his books from class to class while he walked on his crutches.

After a while everybody got so used to seeing me or Shea, or sometimes Jacob, with Skeets that they forgot to be afraid of him. Just as the Truelanders started forgetting to turn their backs on me.

At first Skeets grumbled that the crutches were spoiling the reputation it had taken him years to build, but after a day or two he decided the crutches weren't all bad. "They make it pretty easy to trip up kids that get in my way," he told Shea one day as we were going through the lunch line.

"You're awful," Shea said. "I don't know why we bother to help you at all."

"Because you're afraid not to," Skeets growled.

"You haven't changed a bit," Shea told him crossly, but I could tell she was trying not to smile.

Still, in some way, it was true. Skeets hadn't changed that much. The fact was that he'd never been as mean as we'd thought he was.

Changing wasn't that easy. I knew. I went out to the bridge a couple of times a week and just sat and stared at it. In time I knew I'd have to walk out on it again. I needed to kill my fear of it and all the bridges in my past. Not for Dad. Not even for Shea. But for myself.

It was a slow process changing the way I felt, but I was making progress. At home I could climb up to the sixth rung of the ladder before my knees began locking up.

Shea knew what I was doing, but she didn't try

to help me. Now that I was fighting it myself she knew she didn't have to push me anymore. Still, sometimes she came and sat with me by the bridge, and just having her there with me made me know I'd be able to do it someday.

NOVELS FROM AVON FLARE

CLASS PICTURES 61408-1/$2.95 US/$3.50 Can

Marilyn Sachs

Pat, always the popular one, and shy, plump Lolly have been best friends since kindergarten, through thick and thin, supporting each other during crises. But everything changes when Lolly turns into a thin, pretty blonde and Pat finds herself playing second fiddle for the first time.

BABY SISTER 70358-1/$3.50 US/$4.25 Can

Marilyn Sachs

Her sister was everything Penny could never be, until Penny found something else.

THE GROUNDING OF GROUP 6 83386-7/$3.99 US/$4.99 Can

Julian Thompson

What do parents do when they realize that their sixteen-year old son or daughter is a loser and an embarrassment to the family? Five misfits find they've been set up to disappear at exclusive Coldbrook School, but aren't about to allow themselves to be permanently "grounded.".

TAKING TERRI MUELLER 79004-1/$3.50 US/$4.25 Can

Norma Fox Mazer

Was it possible to be kidnapped by your own father? Terri's father has always told her that her mother died in a car crash—but now Terri has reason to suspect differently, and she struggles to find the truth on her own.

WHEN DOES THE FUN START? 76129-7/$3.50 US/$4.25 Can

Jean Thesman

Nothing has been any fun for Teddy Gideon since she spotted Zack, the love of her life, gazing into the eyes of another girl— a beautiful girl Teddy has never seen before.

Avon Flare Presents
Award-winning Author
JEAN THESMAN

WHEN DOES THE FUN START?

76129-7/$3.50 US/$4.25 Can

Nothing has been any fun for Teddy Gideon since she spotted Zack, the love of her life, gazing into the eyes of another girl—a beautiful girl Teddy has never seen before.

WHO SAID LIFE IS FAIR?

75088-0/$3.50 US/$4.25 Can

Sixteen-year-old Teddy Gideon just can't believe that her plans for a *spectacular* junior year of high school are falling apart.

And Don't Miss:
WAS IT SOMETHING I SAID?

75462-2/$2.75 US/$3.25 Can

COULDN'T I START OVER?

75717-6/$2.95 US/$3.50 Can

THE LAST APRIL DANCERS

70614-8/$2.75 US/$3.50 Can

APPOINTMENT WITH A STRANGER

70864-7/$3.50 US/$4.25 Can